"No reason to think there's anything gruesome in that storage container..."

Jane charged toward it. Tim caught up to her. "Allow me to do the honors."

He bobbled the key in his palm. Jane could think he just wanted to take control of the search, but his instincts made him leery of what...or whom they might find in there.

Tim shoved the key into the container lock and clicked it open. Then he grabbed the door handle, yanking it up.

As the metal squealed, Jane screamed, "Look out! Get back!"

Her warning was too late. As Tim scrambled to stop the door's upward progress, a trip wire dangled from the bottom of the door.

He had no chance of stopping it, so he did the next best thing.

He launched himself backward, covering his face with his arm just before the explosion lifted him and Jane off their feet and threw them to the ground...

DOCKSIDE DANGER

CAROL ERICSON

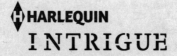

HARLEQUIN
INTRIGUE

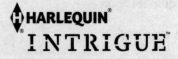

ISBN-13: 978-1-335-58235-5

Dockside Danger

Recycling programs
for this product may
not exist in your area.

Harlequin Enterprises ULC
22 Adelaide St. West, 41st Floor
Toronto, Ontario M5H 4E3, Canada
www.Harlequin.com

Printed in U.S.A.

Carol Ericson is a bestselling, award-winning author of more than forty books. She has an eerie fascination for true crime stories, a love of film noir and a weakness for reality TV, all of which fuel her imagination to create her own tales of murder, mayhem and mystery. To find out more about Carol and her current projects, please visit her website at www.carolericson.com, "where romance flirts with danger."

Books by Carol Ericson

Harlequin Intrigue

The Lost Girls

Canyon Crime Scene
Lakeside Mystery
Dockside Danger

A Kyra and Jake Investigation

The Setup
The Decoy
The Bait
The Trap

Visit the Author Profile page at Harlequin.com.

CAST OF CHARACTERS

Tim Ruskin—An FBI special agent, he has a personal interest in a case he's working involving human trafficking, and things get even more personal when he discovers the LAPD homicide detective in charge is a woman who thinks he's done her wrong.

Jane Falco—This LAPD homicide detective believes that Tim Ruskin used her once before to get information about a case, and she's not going to let him do it again...if only getting used by Tim didn't feel so good.

Natalya Petrova—The murder of this Russian immigrant plunges Jane into the world of the Russian mob, but Natalya is not just an innocent victim.

Austin Walker—Natalya's boyfriend may be guilty of her murder, or he may have information that just might get him killed, too.

Lana Savchenko—The sister of Tim's friend has been missing for months. Is he too late to save her from the traffickers?

Damon Carter—Jane's partner takes a lot of time off and she bends over backward to accommodate him, but is his time off really personal or is he hiding a secret from her?

Ivan Kozlov—The owner of a popular Russian restaurant in Hollywood, he has connections to the mob and knows more than he's willing to admit.

Chapter One

FBI Special Agent Tim Ruskin flattened his body against the metal wall of the warehouse, his nose twitching at the smells of rot and urine coming from the corners of the building. He shifted, and his knee pinged the corner of a cage. The rage he'd felt the first time he entered this space rushed back through his body, and his chest prickled with heat. He didn't want to imagine Lana…or anyone else, trapped in here.

A pen light flashed twice from across the room. Tim tensed and reached for his weapon. As he curled his fingers around the cold, hard metal of his gun, he set his jaw in determination. He'd shoot to kill if one of these cockroaches even touched a weapon.

The warehouse door rattled, and Tim coiled his muscles. He gritted his teeth at the sound of screeching metal as the door cracked open. A single beam from a flashlight fell across the floor, illuminating nothing but the dirty cement.

Tim held his breath, willing the intruder to enter with more than a flashlight in his hand. The door swung wider, and the silhouette of a man appeared in the en-

trance. The figure hissed and then coughed as he shuffled into the warehouse, dragging something on wheels
behind him.

Tim's eyes watered from the strain as he peered into
the darkness behind the man. Where were the others?
His finger twitched on the trigger.

The man entering the warehouse whistled an off-key
tune and turned to his right to grab the lever that would
flood the space with light—only it wouldn't. Tim and
his team had made sure of that. The intruder slammed
the lever upward and nothing happened. He swore in
Spanish.

Spanish? Tim licked his dry lips, and his gaze
shifted to his left as if his team member had an expla-
nation for the different language. Would the stranger's
cohorts follow him inside now to investigate the lighting situation?

The man tried the lever again with the same results.
He flicked his flashlight at the ceiling, as if he could
find the answer there among the fluorescent tubes lined
up like dormant soldiers awaiting orders. Then the intruder kicked the item he'd dragged in behind him and
metal clanged in the recesses of the warehouse.

Tim stiffened. What the hell had he brought with
him? Another cage? More restraints?

Nobody else had followed the man inside the warehouse. He hadn't addressed anyone outside. The knots in
Tim's gut tightened. Even if they nailed just one of these
bastards, he could work with that. There were ways of
getting people to talk, to rat out their associates…and
Tim had used them all.

The man turned toward the door, and Tim made his move. They couldn't let him walk out. "Stop! Hands up!"

Light flooded the space as one of the agents turned on a spotlight, but the intruder didn't wait to see what was waiting for him inside. He lunged for the door and slammed it behind him.

Tim yelled. "I got him. I got him."

He sprinted toward the door and flung it open. As he lurched outside, he tripped over the bucket the man had left in his path. Why did the man bring a bucket to a prison?

Tim looked up as he scrambled to his feet just in time to see the man galloping across the parking lot toward the boat slips. They might have a speedboat ready. He couldn't lose him to the water. They may never get this chance again.

Tim lengthened his stride, closing the gap between them. He muttered, "C'mon. Come at me with a gun."

The figure began to falter as he neared the water's edge. Maybe his companions had left him high and dry.

Tim thrust his gun in front of him as he slowed his pace. "Stop! On the ground, or I shoot."

The man hesitated, turned his head for a final look at Tim and then went into the water.

Tim swore…in English. He dropped his weapon on the edge of the dock and jumped in after the struggling figure splashing and gulping water, not even making an effort to swim away.

He grabbed the man's clothing, his hands feeling for a weapon. The guy fought against him, but he was fighting against the water, too, and finally figured Tim was the better bet.

Tim hauled him to the side of the slip, his breath coming out in short spurts. "Crawl up there and stay on your stomach."

Tim grabbed his own gun and hoisted himself out of the brackish water that felt oily against his skin. He aimed it at the man as he dragged himself onto the slip, flattening onto his belly, his dark hair plastered to his skull, his moustache dripping water like a walrus's.

The suspect coughed and spluttered. "*Señor, señor,* please don't shoot."

"You can cut the act. You're under arrest for human trafficking, and I'm sure a helluva lot more." Tim released the cuffs from his belt and jingled them as he shook them out. Maybe this man could tell him about Lana.

"Traffic, what? *Señor,* I there to clean the building."

"To clean the building?" Tim stared into the man's dark, frightened eyes, the whites shining clear in the moonlight, and knew he was telling the truth.

His gut roiled and he fell back on his hands. They'd missed the Bratva again…and this time he knew someone had tipped them off.

DETECTIVE JANE FALCO dropped her purse in the bottom drawer of her desk and locked the drawer. Pretty sad when you had to lock up your purse in the Homicide Division of the LAPD, but she didn't want to take any chances. She hadn't been here long enough to assess her coworkers' trustworthiness, and she'd gone through too much at Pacific Division to let down her guard. She patted the locked drawer. Better safe than sorry.

Lieutenant Figueroa burst into the room, waving a piece of paper. "You're up, Falco. Where's Carter?"

"Some personal business, LT." With the key still in her hand, Jane unlocked her desk drawer and grabbed her purse. "Another domestic?"

"Seems like it. Body of a woman located in her bathtub. Boyfriend nowhere to be found." The lieutenant cocked his head at her. "Show some enthusiasm, Falco. You're good at these."

"Because I'm a woman?" She hitched her purse over her shoulder and snatched the info sheet out of Fig's hand. He didn't know about her personal background, so it couldn't be that.

Figueroa rolled his eyes. "Word of advice, Falco. Lose the chip on your shoulder. You'll fit in a lot better here."

"Yes, sir." She nodded once, flicked her ponytail over her shoulder and breezed past him on her way to her third domestic in seven weeks.

Not that she didn't find satisfaction in solving these cases and bringing the perpetrator to justice, but *solving* was a generous term for what she did. Typically, all the evidence screamed out at her, pointing her in the direction of the husband or the boyfriend or the ex. Flipping through the restraining orders and the X-rays of previous broken bones and listening to the 911 calls made her blood boil. By the time she got involved, it was too late for the victim.

It had almost been too late for Mom.

On her way to the victim's house in Hollywood, she called her partner and left him a voice mail about the case they'd caught. Carter had been out to lunch the past few months dealing with an ugly custody battle. Seemed his ex wasn't too happy with Damon moving on with a new girlfriend. Jane had kept his secrets and his absences to herself. The surest way to draw attention to herself at the Northeast Division would be to rat out her partner. She didn't mind his absenteeism, anyway. She preferred working alone.

When she pulled up to the sad little tract house in North Hollywood, she scanned the clutches of people on the sidewalk gawking at the commotion of police cars and yellow crime scene tape. She predicted tales of drunkenness and cruelty from the neighbors. If they all had known this would happen—and that was what they'd claim—why didn't anyone do anything to help the woman?

Jane huffed out a sigh and grabbed her jacket from the back seat. Once out of the car, she slid her arms into the sleeves of the jacket and smoothed it over the gun on her hip.

Flashing her badge at the officer manning the perimeter, she ducked under the tape and approached a fresh-faced uniform perched on the first step of the porch, wiping the back of his hand across his mouth.

She studied the green tinge to his face and raised her eyebrows behind her sunglasses. "Bad?"

"Yes, ma'am." He swallowed and then widened his eyes, wishing he hadn't.

"Are you sick…" she peered at his name tag "…Officer Tran?"

"No, no, ma'am." He pulled back his shoulders.

She jerked her thumb over her shoulder. "If you feel the urge, do it around the corner of the house."

"Y-yes, ma'am."

Jane plucked her sunglasses from her face and dropped them into her jacket pocket as she stepped across the threshold of the messy house. She could taste the metallic scent of blood on the back of her tongue, but she didn't make the same mistake as Tran by swallowing. That only made it worse.

A sergeant stood guard at the hallway to the back rooms, although by the looks of things the victim didn't need protection anymore.

He nodded at her. "Sergeant Washington, Detective Falco."

"You've got a nauseous officer on the porch, Sergeant." She snapped on her gloves.

"Tran's a newbie, Falco. I think this is his first homicide…" he tipped his head toward the open door he was blocking with his muscled frame "…and it ain't pretty."

"It never is." She approached him, and they did a little dance in the hallway to trade places. "Have you talked to any of the neighbors, yet?"

"Just the one next door, who said the victim, Natalya Petrova, lived here with her boyfriend—Austin Walker. He's nowhere to be found."

She jerked her head toward the front of the house, her ponytail swinging to one side. "Is that the neighbor who called it in?"

"Maybe. Anonymous call to 911. Told us what we might find." He lifted his big shoulders. "Could've been the boyfriend calling it in, feeling guilty."

"We'll find out soon enough when we trace that call—if we can. Do you know if the caller had a Russian accent?"

"I didn't hear the call and nobody said."

"How'd you ID the victim?"

"Neighbor told us her name. Sort of butchered the last name, but we checked the purse in the living room and got her license."

Jane's gaze flicked to the bathroom behind Washington and zeroed in on a streak of blood running down the wall. More than Natalya's last name had been butchered.

The tinny odor of the woman's blood saturated the air, and Jane put her gloved hand over her nose and mouth for a second. "Thanks, Sergeant. Start canvassing the neighbors. I'll have a look at the scene before the CSI team gets here."

Washington ambled out of the house, and Jane stepped into the bathroom, her gaze darting from the sink to the toilet to the shower, its curtain printed with mermaids firmly drawn across the tub/shower combo. Nothing in this small bathroom, cluttered with makeup and hair products, indicated a struggle. The living room hadn't been pristine, but no signs of a life-and-death battle in there, either.

Jane shuffled forward and hooked a finger on the shower curtain, the mermaids shivering at her touch.

She eased it to the side, and the shower curtain hooks clacked like disapproving tongues.

Her gaze dropped to the tub. She'd expected water, but the young woman with the gash across her throat and the multiple stab wounds to her chest and abdomen lounged in an empty tub, her hair dry, except for the blood that matted it against her nude body and the porcelain behind her. A tattoo of one of those Russian nesting dolls on her thigh was the only splash of color that wasn't blood.

Crouching next to the bathtub, Jane murmured, "Did your boyfriend do this do you, Natalya? Did he do this after claiming he loved you more than anything in the world?"

"Detective Falco?"

Jane cranked her head over her shoulder without an ounce of embarrassment at being caught talking to the murder victim. Sometimes when you talked to the dead, they told you things. "Hey, Lori. Is the rest of Forensics here?"

The young fingerprint tech nodded, her gaze avoiding the mess in the tub. "They are. You ready?"

"Not yet." Jane scratched her chin against her shoulder, not wanting to touch her own face with her gloved fingers. "Have you started dusting for prints, yet?"

"I'm going to start in the bedroom. There's a glass on the nightstand in there and a lot of other junk, but no evidence of a struggle."

"Give me a few more minutes. I'll grab the team when I'm done. Coroner van here, yet?"

"Nope." Lori covered her face with her hands. "There must be a lot of blood in that tub."

"A river."

Lori cranked her head over her shoulder and called out to the others. "Detective Falco isn't done yet."

As Lori backed away from the bathroom door, Jane turned her attention back to the woman in the tub. She slid a finger beneath Natalya's wrist and lifted her hand, studying her neatly clipped fingernails. No broken nails and nothing beneath them—not that she could see. The CSI would bag the hands and check the fingernails for skin cells not visible to Jane's cursory examination.

She skimmed a finger along Natalya's hand. "You didn't fight back, girl? Did he take you by surprise?"

Jane couldn't see any injuries on Natalya's body other than the obvious fatal wounds—no bruising on her face, no contusions to the head, no purple necklace of prints around her neck.

How did Natalya's killer manage to get her into a dry tub, naked, and slash her without disrupting anything else in the house? Even if Natalya had been in here ready to take a shower, she'd have tried to avoid the knife, pulling down the shower curtain or bumping her head and suffering defensive wounds on her arms.

Of course, if she knew her assailant and had welcomed him into the tub with her, she never would've had a chance to react after he slashed her throat from behind—which brought her back to the boyfriend.

Jane took a few of her own pictures and recorded some observations before relinquishing the space to the

CSIs. She gave her summary to them before emerging into the hallway and taking a big breath.

She caught Lori's sleeve as the fingerprint tech joined the crowd in the bathroom. "Any signs of a break-in that you could see? Any bloody prints on the doors or windows?"

"No blood, prints or otherwise, in the rest of the house. One of the officers said all the doors and windows were locked." Lori's jaw tightened. "It was probably the boyfriend."

Lori would know a thing or two about that, as her own brother was in prison for murdering his girlfriend. Why did everyone with violence in their pasts manage to find jobs where they could relive it every day?

Jane said, "Probably open-and-shut."

She scooted past Lori and stood with her hands on her hips, surveying the living room. How did Natalya's boyfriend manage to get out of the house after that carnage without leaving a trace of blood? He must've changed in the bathroom, bagged his bloody clothes and the murder weapon and walked out of here without leaving any evidence. Hardly the crime of passion that usually accompanied these cases. Typically, domestics didn't involve a whole lot of planning.

She stepped onto the porch and took a bigger breath. This one actually included some fresh air. She peeled off her gloves and nudged Tran's shoulder. "Feeling better, Tran?"

The officer wiped his hands on his slacks. "A little. I'm past the puking stage, anyway."

"Progress." She took her sunglasses out of her pocket

and clapped them onto her face. Peering through the lenses, she spotted Sergeant Washington on the sidewalk talking to a woman gesticulating wildly. Looked like he had a live one.

She joined the sergeant on the sidewalk. "Is this a witness?"

The woman turned her protruding blue eyes on Jane. "I didn't see anything…this time, but those two are always fighting. I seen him shove her around before."

"Are you talking about Natalya's boyfriend?"

"Austin Walker, that's him." The neighbor crossed her arms over an ample breast and hunched her shoulders.

Washington edged away, leaving Jane to deal with the woman.

Jane fished a notepad out of her pocket. "Your name, ma'am?"

"June Horman."

"And you live next door to Natalya and Austin?"

She pointed a finger with chipped red polish on the nail to the run-down stucco bungalow next to Natalya's house. "Right there."

"Did you know the deceased well? Her boyfriend?"

June blinked her pale lashes. "Not really, just to wave. One time we had a good jolt out here from an earthquake, and the Russian girl got all excited."

"He wasn't Russian, though, the boyfriend?"

"No." June's thin lips twisted. "He was a biker type—long hair, leather jacket, tattoos. I always thought he might be dealing drugs in there. People coming and going—*women* coming and going."

"We'll certainly take a look." Jane slipped a card out of her pocket. "If you think of anything else, June, give me a call."

"I will." She clasped her hands in front of her. "Poor little thing. How'd she die?"

"I can't tell you that, June. Thanks for the information."

Jane talked to several other neighbors, hitting the ones Washington had missed. Before the sergeant left, he handed over his notes on his interviews.

He rolled his big shoulders. "Nobody saw anything. Time of death must've been last night, right?"

"As far as I can tell. The coroner will have more." She shoved her glasses to the top of her head. "Thanks for helping out here today."

"Where's your partner?"

"On other business." She pivoted toward the house. "I'm going to talk to the CSIs and the medical examiner before I leave."

She scooped in a few more breaths of fresh air before ducking into the house again. Nobody could tell her much more than she'd gleaned herself. The rest of the investigation would take place in the labs and on the computers. Her first order of business would be finding Austin. Already looked bad for him that he wasn't at home and hadn't reported the murder.

After Jane checked in with the lieutenant and her partner had put out an all-points bulletin on Austin's car, she packed up her files and laptop. She could finish working at home.

A half hour later, she left the freeway and took the

winding road to her home in Benedict Canyon with ease. She'd lived here long enough to have every turn and bump memorized, even in the dark—she usually arrived home after nightfall.

She didn't feel one ounce of guilt getting this house in the divorce from Aaron. It had always been more hers than his, anyway. He'd hated the isolation, hated being away from the bright lights, big city. He'd managed to work his way back to the excitement he craved, even before they separated.

Yeah, Aaron owed her this house. She'd let him off easy.

She pulled into the driveway that dipped toward the house. The front, shrouded with trees, looked foreboding, but the back of the house faced a canyon, the open space flooding the rooms with light during the day.

She parked and grabbed her bag and jacket from the front passenger seat. Her low heels crunched on the gravel that led to her front porch. A shadow moved to her right behind the bushes that gave the house its rustic aspect.

Always in hyperalert mode, Jane felt the hair on the back of her neck quiver. She dropped her bag and pulled her gun from her waistband.

Aiming it at the bushes, she growled. "Give me one reason why I shouldn't shoot you."

The shadow took shape as it stepped from its cover. The man held out both of his hands. "It's Tim Ruskin, Jane."

All her senses percolated, and she cocked her head. "Give me another reason."

Chapter Two

Tim clenched his teeth for a second. She hadn't forgiven him. He edged into the light spilling from the fixture over her porch, spreading his arms. "Okay, how about, I'm not armed?"

Her eyes glowed at him in the dark, and he remembered gazing into their tawny depths before they'd narrowed at him in distrust.

She snorted, lowering her weapon. "I don't believe for one minute you're not strapped."

He broadened his stance and spread his jacket. "It's on me, but not in my hand."

"Technicalities." She holstered her gun. "What are you doing here?"

She wasn't going to make this easy, and he didn't blame her. "That's obvious. I came here to see you."

"Yeah, that part's obvious." She picked up her bag and hitched it over her shoulder. "What do you want?"

She'd already turned her back on him and had her keys out to unlock her front door.

He had to make this good for her to even listen to him and not slam the door in his face. He cleared his throat. "It's about the case you caught this afternoon—Natalya Petrova."

She'd opened the door, but Natalya's name had her turning slowly, her nostrils flaring. "How the hell do you know about that case? I just got it today."

"C'mon, Jane." He bumped his chest with his fist. "I'm FBI."

"Oh, is that who you are this time?" She pushed through the door and stood guard at the entrance. "No role playing? No lying?"

"Can we just talk, Jane?" He rubbed his chin. "We're on the same side here. We both want to find out who killed Natalya."

When her lashes fluttered and her bottom lip quivered, he knew he had her. Jane never wanted to let down a victim, and she'd work with the devil himself to solve a case—and it seemed he didn't rate any higher in her estimation than Lucifer.

"Why is the FBI interested in a case of domestic violence?" She wedged one hand on the door and the other on the doorjamb, blocking his entrance.

"Natalya's death may be something else. We're not on this officially. I just want to know what you found out there today."

"At least you're knocking on my door, asking, this time. You're making progress, Ruskin." She flicked her sleek ponytail over her shoulder. "I guess you figured even a dumb cop could be fooled only once."

As her thick, dark hair swung behind her, he swallowed. His fingers tingled with the memory of loosening her mane from its confinement and burying his face in the fragrant locks.

He blinked when he realized the opening of the doorway was getting smaller. He stuck his foot in the space. "Are you fishing to get me to say you're not a dumb cop? I think you're top-notch, and that's why I wanted to work with you."

"Work with me? Is that what you called that trickery?" She raised her eyebrows, but at least she hadn't shut him out, yet.

He pointed over her shoulder to the warm space inside. "Can you let me in, so we can talk about this like two professionals?"

She sighed, her shoulders sagging in defeat, as if this had been a contest. "Whatever."

Jane turned and walked into her house, leaving the door open behind her. Tim stepped over the threshold and pulled the door closed. He locked the dead bolt on the top. If Jane weren't a cop with a .38 Special, he'd think she was unwise for living in this isolated spot alone. But Jane always had something to prove. It was what had torn them apart in the end—no matter what she said.

While she banged around in the kitchen, Tim strolled to the window overlooking the canyon—dark now, with a few pinpoints of light where other houses nestled in their solitude. His reflection shimmered back at him.

"No wildfires lately?"

"None affecting me." She poked her head out from

the kitchen. "Do you want something to drink? Water? Coffee?"

"I'm good, but you probably haven't had dinner yet, so go ahead with what you were planning."

She held up a bottle of red wine by the neck. "After the day I had, I'm planning this."

She hadn't offered him any of that—not that he was much of a wine drinker. Maybe she'd remembered that about him. He remembered so much about her.

"Go ahead." Wedging a shoulder against the window, he crossed his arms and waited while she poured herself a glass.

She emerged from the kitchen with her wine in one hand and a file folder in the other. Sitting on one edge of her couch, facing the window, she asked, "Why is the FBI interested in the murder of Natalya Petrova?"

He took a seat across from her in a deep-cushioned chair, trying to perch on the edge. You couldn't let your guard down with Jane Falco for a minute. "She has some associations with…people we know."

"I'm aware of the kind of people the FBI knows. You're talking about Bratva…the Russian criminal element. You think they had something to do with Natalya's death?"

"We don't, not yet." Tim rubbed his hands together. "I'd just like to know what you found in her house today."

Jane swirled her wine and took a careful sip. "You're here unofficially, aren't you? You found out somehow that I caught the case and figured you could sweet-talk your way into some information."

A muscle twitched at the corner of his eye, and he rubbed it. "I'm just asking you, Jane. There is no sweet talk involved."

"That's a change for you." She took another swig of her wine—this one not so careful. It stained her soft lips.

"That was not sweet talk before, either. I'm sorry I didn't tell you I was undercover, but those feelings?" He slammed his fist against his knee. "Those were real."

Gazing into her glass, she parted her lips, and he could detect a slight tremble to her mouth. "It was so convenient, though, wasn't it? Get close to the detective and you could find out all kinds of things from the LAPD they wouldn't normally reveal to the FBI."

"There should be more cooperation between us, and there wouldn't be any need for subterfuge."

Her eyebrows jumped. "So you're admitting there *was* subterfuge?"

"That's not what I meant." He ran a hand across his face, all of a sudden feeling exhausted. "We work well together and you know it. If you don't want to tell me what you found in Natalya's house, I'll try to get the information another way."

She dropped the file folder on the coffee table between them. "There are some pictures of the crime scene in there—not pretty, made a grown man puke. Looks like her killer caught her in the act of starting a bath or shower. She was undressed, but there was no water in the tub, no struggle in the bathroom. The coroner can tell us if the slit to her throat came from behind. Maybe she knew her killer, was talking to him in the bathroom, and he came at her from behind and sliced her throat. Once he had her incapacitated, if not deceased, in the tub, he proceeded to stab her chest and abdomen multiple times for good measure, or out of rage. Points to the boyfriend, who's nowhere to be found."

He slid the folder toward him with one finger and flipped it open. His gaze flicked over Natalya in the tub, bloodied and decidedly dead, and tried not to see Lana in her place. "No defensive wounds?"

"None that I could see. No upset in the house, either. No signs of a break-in."

"She knew her killer." He shuffled through the rest of the photos, the knots tightening in his gut. "She can't be more than twenty-one."

"She turned twenty-four a few weeks ago." Jane tossed back her wine and ran her tongue along her upper lip. "We found her purse, wallet and driver's license. But we can't find her boyfriend—and he's not Russian."

Tim sealed his lips. Austin Walker *was* Russian, but he didn't want to raise any red flags with Jane that he knew too much about the victim.

He pretended to study the rest of the notes in the folder, watching Jane out of the corner of his eye. "How's the new gig at the Northeast Division going?"

"I've been pigeonholed already." She lifted her

shoulders. "But at least they don't know I was duped by an undercover FBI agent, unless the previous bunch I worked with informed them and they all shared a good laugh."

He shoved the folder away from him, and a picture of Natalya slid to the floor, facedown. He huffed out a breath before continuing. "How are they pigeonholing you and why?"

"Domestics." She tapped a finger on the file. "I'm the queen of domestics now—open-and-shut cases."

"How is that a bad thing?" He jerked his thumb over his shoulder. "Can I get some water?"

"Help yourself. The bad thing—" she curled one leg beneath her "—is that they don't seem to trust me with anything more complex than a domestic. There's no real investigation work. The suspect is obvious. He's usually no criminal mastermind, so he leaves lots of clues and most of the time he confesses."

He took a glass from the cupboard and pressed it against the lever on the fridge door. "I still don't see the downside. You get justice for the victim and take a dirtbag off the street."

"You're purposely misunderstanding me. Of course I'm thrilled to put these guys behind bars. Somebody has to do it, but why is it always me? It's like the brass doesn't trust a woman to investigate any other type of homicide." Jane stood up, clutching her wineglass as if she were ready to throw the remnants in someone's face. "What are you really doing here, Tim? What do you know about Natalya?"

He gulped his water. "Her name came up in an investigation we're working in LA. We have a flag on her, so when her homicide popped up on our radar, we took notice. The Bureau gave me the assignment to look into her death before I even knew you caught the case. Honestly, I didn't even know you'd left Pacific Division."

"And when you found out I was lead detective on the case?" She strolled into the kitchen, brushing past him.

"I was…glad. I've been wanting to see you for a while." He leaned back against the counter next to where she was rinsing her glass in the sink. "You look great. I like what you did with your hair."

With wet fingers, she pinched the ends of her dark brown locks, a rose tint to her cheeks. "I just…my friend gave me this combination hairbrush and blow-dryer thing to straighten it."

Jane had always downplayed her looks, earning her the nickname of Plain Jane at Pacific. The other detectives said it behind her back, but she knew about it… and liked it. She'd cultivated that look by scooping her unruly hair into a messy bun at the nape of her neck, hiding her spectacular tawny-hued eyes with oversize glasses and outfitting her tall, lean frame in mannish suits that hung on her body, concealing her soft curves.

He almost hadn't recognized the woman tonight illuminated by her porch light, a stylish suit outlining her slim, athletic body, a V-neck blouse exposing her long neck and those eyes, flashing fire from beneath a pair of contact lenses.

Those eyes darkened now as they met his, the blush spreading on her cheeks.

Reaching up, he wound a strand of her hair around his finger. "It's beautiful, but I kinda liked those wayward curls."

He wasn't a particularly tall man and Jane, even without her low-heeled boots stashed by the side of the couch, met him nose to nose. Perfect height for an easy kiss.

His phone buzzed in his pocket, breaking the spell, and Jane jerked her head back to the sink. He should've known—nothing was easy with Jane Falco.

Backing away from her, he said, "I gotta take this."

He tapped to answer. "Just a second, Kyle."

He pointed to the French doors that led to her patio and the wild canyon beneath it. She nodded, her mouth tightening into a thin line.

He pulled open one door and stepped into the cool evening. He inhaled the scent of sticky-sweet pine and said, "What's going on, Kyle?"

"We located the boyfriend."

"Is he dead?" Tim watched Jane through the glass as she returned to the living room and straightened the pillow on the couch and the coaster that had just hosted her wineglass. She was getting ready to kick him out.

Kyle answered with a growl. "Not yet. LAPD investigating as a domestic?"

"So far."

"Good. Let's keep it that way."

Kyle ended the call before Tim could respond. He

cupped the phone between his hands, his gaze tracking Jane in the warm light, beyond his reach.

This case would push her even further away from him, unless he made some changes to his behavior. He dropped the phone in his pocket, plastered a smile on his face and got ready to lie…again.

Chapter Three

With nervous hands, Jane fluffed a cushion as Tim returned from the patio, bringing a huff of fresh air with him and a fake smile on his face.

"Work?"

"Always." He slipped the cell phone in his pocket, as if afraid she could still hear the call.

"Natalya's case?" She flicked a lock of hair over her shoulder, trying to rid herself of his touch, wishing for the scraped-back look of the severe ponytail she'd loosened in the car on the way home. Why had she babbled on like an idiot about the blow-dryer brush Amy had given her? That was what happened when you let your hair down.

"Nah." He waved his arm expansively. "Some other case."

She dipped and picked up Natalya's picture from the floor. Pinching the top of the photo with two fingers, she hung it out, facing him. "All done with her, then?"

"I'll leave the case in your capable hands. You'll find the boyfriend, make it stick and put him away. Another win for the good guys." He turned his back on her and Natalya and headed for the kitchen. Holding up his empty water glass, he said, "Thanks for the...hospitality."

Her lips quirked into a half smile. "You have low standards."

He glanced at her over his shoulder as he bent to place the glass in the dishwasher, his backside looking way too good in those jeans. "My standards have always been very high."

The sex appeal came off him in waves, and she braced herself for the deluge—but it never worked that way with Tim. Instead of the onslaught, an insinuating curl of sensuality whispered around her body until it found its way through her pores, soaking her in want, leaving her knees weak.

She closed her eyes for a second, reveling in the sensation. Most FBI guys she knew were nerds. That was why she hadn't made him as a Fibbie—at least that was what she'd told herself.

The Bureau usually hired accounting, legal and cyber geeks with their pressed khakis and neat ties that you could pick out a mile away. Occasionally, they let a wolf through the doors, someone dangerous and unpredictable. Tim was that wolf.

That was probably why he'd been so good undercover. He had a dangerous side—a side that had meshed seamlessly with his alter ego, Terry Rush. She hadn't let him explain himself once she'd discovered his deception. Now she wondered about his past.

She coughed and brushed the goose bumps from her arms. "If you think a glass of water you had to get yourself and some pictures of a dead girl are hospitality, wait until you stay at the Ritz."

The shadow of a smile flickered across his mouth. "I've taken up enough of your time tonight. I'm sure you're…busy." His gaze wandered across her neat, cozy house—the neatness reflecting her to a T, the coziness not so much—and she knew that he knew damned well she had no business, no game, no life.

"I *am* busy." She started for the front door, because someone had to make a move. "You'll keep me posted if you hear anything more about Natalya? Maybe her murder had nothing to do with her missing boyfriend and everything to do with your Russian friends."

Tim's step faltered as he followed her to the door. "I don't think so, Jane. I believe you got yourself another domestic. Go get 'em, girl."

She gave him a wide berth to reach the door, so she wouldn't have to feel the warmth and pull of his body.

He made a half-turn and thought better of it, sailing onto the porch with a wave of his hand.

Jane stepped outside and watched the darkness envelop Tim as he sauntered down her driveway to the shadowy street where he'd parked his car to surprise her. Away from his supercharged presence, Jane took a deep breath of the pine-scented air to clear her brain, as the cool breeze prickled her skin.

FBI Special Agent Tim Ruskin was lying through his perfect teeth.

THE FOLLOWING MORNING, Jane cupped both hands around her coffee mug and surveyed the living room from a stool at the kitchen island. As she squinted her eyes, she could almost imagine Tim had never been in her space. Then her lashes flew open, and she could make out the impression his back had left on one of her cushions and could catch his masculine scent in the kitchen air, hovering just beneath the freshly ground coffee beans.

She hopped from the stool, her coffee sloshing over the rim, and pounded her fist into the cushion. Then she snagged her jacket from the back of a chair and flew out the front door, slamming it behind her on Tim's presence in her house and her foolish feelings.

When she reached the station, Damon was already at his desk, hunched forward, his eyes glued to his computer monitor.

Without looking up, he said, "Thanks for covering for me yesterday."

"Did you get everything settled?" She pulled out her chair and sat at her desk next to him.

"Not really." He finally dragged his gaze away from his computer and slumped in his seat. "It's not enough Denise is getting half my pension when I retire, she wants me to keep paying for the house."

"Sounds like you need a better attorney. Are you using Terrence Hicks? I hear he's the man." Jane shrugged out of her jacket.

"He's out of my price range. They all are." Damon cocked his head at her. "Did you use him?"

"I didn't have to. Aaron was more than generous, and we didn't have kids." And she'd had something over his head.

Damon leaned in close and cupped a hand around his mouth. "The advantages to marrying a gazillionaire."

"Yeah, one of just a few." She'd opened up to Damon about her marriage and divorce. Her partner had needed the support and she'd needed to cultivate more goodwill and closeness with her colleagues. Nobody had had her back at Pacific Division, and she took half the blame for that.

She asked, "Did you get a chance to catch up?"

"I did. Thanks for emailing the info. Still no luck on the whereabouts of Austin Walker. No location on his car through license plate readers, either. But let's face it—" Damon smoothed one hand over his shaved head "—his silence is deafening. If your woman is dead or you can't reach her, wouldn't you call the police?"

"Unless he's hurt. Maybe someone killed Natalya and abducted Austin or injured him." Jane tucked a strand of hair behind her ear. Tim had noticed her hair...and liked it.

"Again, if he's hurt, you'd think he'd call the police." Damon drummed his fingers on the desk. "Unless someone killed Natalya because of Austin and he doesn't want to fess up to the cops."

"Did you discover anything in his background?" She'd given Damon Austin's details and had asked him to do some research.

"Not yet." Damon gestured to the computer. "Was digging in when you got here. He doesn't have a criminal record, so if he's dealing or is into anything else illegal, we don't know about it."

She tapped his empty cup. "You want a refill?"

He nodded and as she turned away with both of their cups in her hands, she almost bumped into Detective Marino.

His ruddy face spread into a smile. "Hey, Carter, I heard you and Falco caught another domestic. At this rate, you two are gonna forget what it's like to do real detective work."

Jane raised one eyebrow. "You mean like you?"

Damon chuckled as he smacked his desk, and Detective Holt choked on his coffee as he walked by. "She got you there, Marino."

Marino's face got redder and he slouched from the room.

Jane headed for the lunchroom with a little spring in her step. The insults came fast and furious in the detective room, and she'd been practicing her comebacks. That one had hit home. Marino was the laziest detective on the squad, and everyone knew it.

It still didn't soothe the sting of his remark. Everyone must've noticed the types of cases she and Damon worked…and why. Damon was still relatively new, over from Vice, but she didn't have that excuse. She'd worked Homicide at Pacific Division. The lieutenant here needed to trust her more.

She filled up the mugs with coffee, added cream and sweetener to hers and carried them back to the squad room. As she put Damon's next to his mouse, he glanced up.

"I found out something a little unusual about our guy."

"Oh?" She sat in her chair and scooted it close to Damon's.

"He's Russian, like Natalya."

Jane spat her coffee back in her cup. "Austin Walker is Russian?"

"His parents adopted him from Russia when he was ten. He changed his name shortly after he arrived here." He put his finger on the monitor. "Oleg Stepanchikov."

"I'm pretty sure you mangled that last name." She hunched over his shoulder to read the name herself and murmured. "I'll be damned, so he is."

Sitting back, she chewed on her bottom lip. If Tim had Natalya on his radar, did he also have Austin on his radar? If he did, Tim already knew Austin was Russian…and had failed to tell her. She ground her back teeth together. No surprise there.

"Austin being Russian doesn't convict him or let him off the hook, but it's interesting. Don't you think so?"

"Very interesting." She rapped on his desk. "Good work, Damon. Do you want to attend her autopsy?"

Her partner swallowed. "Do I have to?"

"No, but I told the medical examiner's office I wanted to be there when they finish, so I can get some insight firsthand." She tapped her phone. "I just got a text that they got started."

"I'm going to skip this one, if that's okay with you, Jane." He wrinkled his nose. "I know I have to witness one, start to finish, and I plan to do that, but…"

"But your first one doesn't have to be a healthy young woman." She held up a hand. "I get it. You're good. Keep digging on our boy Austin."

Jane worked through lunch, waiting for the call from the coroner. When it came, she glanced at Damon. "Are you sure you don't want to come along?"

Damon held up his hands and wiggled his fingers. "I'm going through the prints at the house that Lori sent over from the lab."

"Okay, I'll give you an update when I get back."

Jane drove to the medical examiner's building downtown and stopped at the desk in front. Flashing her badge, she said, "Dr. Ellis is expecting me in the morgue."

She took the elevator to the basement, and inhaled a deep breath of the antiseptic-scented air in the hallway before entering the room.

Her gaze flicked toward Natalya's body on the stainless-steel slab, and she unclenched her jaw as she nodded to Dr. Ellis. "Thanks for calling me. I wanted to be here in person."

Dr. Ellis removed her glasses. "The cause of death is obvious—the slash across the throat hit the carotid and she bled out quickly into the tub."

"So, no surprises." Jane sawed her lower lip with her teeth. "Natalya must've been very close to her killer to allow him to get right behind her like that—no signs of struggle in the house and no defensive wounds on Natalya."

"I wouldn't say no surprises." Dr. Ellis lifted Natalya's arm. "Do you see that?"

Jane leaned in and studied the pale skin of Natalya's inner arm, marred by lines of purple bruises. She shivered. She'd seen her share of bruises left by the grip of a hand. "Looks like someone may have grabbed her arm."

"Grabbed her arm…" Dr. Ellis's gloved finger circled another tiny blue mark on the inside of Natalya's elbow "…and injected her with something. The tox report will tell us more."

Jane covered her mouth. "You're sure that wasn't self-inflicted? Maybe Natalya is a user."

Dr. Ellis lifted her shoulders in her white lab coat. "Could be, but there are no track marks on her arm, and I couldn't find any telltale pinpricks between her toes or other common injection sites for addicts."

Jane's heart skipped a beat. "That would explain why there was no upset in the house. He got her into that tub and put the knife to her throat because she was already incapacitated."

"That would be my guess, Detective."

Jane said more to herself than the doctor, "If Austin did this, why would he need to drug her first?"

"I'll leave that for you to figure out. As I said, the tox report will tell us more. We'll have that back in a few weeks." Dr. Ellis smoothed Natalya's wet hair back from her pasty forehead. "What are we doing with our girl, Jane?"

Jane's nose stung. "She's from a small town in Siberia. We haven't been able to contact her family, yet."

"Every parent's worst nightmare." Dr. Ellis flicked the white sheet over Natalya's face. "I'll send you the full report."

"Thanks… Elizabeth."

When she got outside, Jane gulped in the fresh air. If Austin didn't do this, where was he?

She'd missed lunch, but her appetite had evaporated. She raced back to the station to update Damon.

On her way upstairs, she passed Detective Jake McAllister. He and his partner, Billy Crouch, were the undisputed superstars of the department. He slowed his gait and asked, "Did you find the boyfriend, yet?"

"Not yet, but this case might not be that simple."

"They rarely are. Keep digging."

Jane jogged up the rest of the stairs. It had to be a sign if J-Mac was encouraging her.

She tossed her jacket on her desk and nudged Damon's chair with her foot. "Looks like Natalya might've been drugged first."

"Really?" Damon twisted his head to the side. "That pokes a hole in the boyfriend-as-killer theory. Why would Austin have to drug her to get close?"

"That was my first thought, but maybe he did it so she wouldn't fight back. Points away from a typical crime of passion." She flicked her fingers at his screen. "Any luck with those prints? If someone other than Austin was involved, we might get lucky."

"Yeah, no luck." He rubbed his forehead with one stubby finger. "No latent prints in blood at all. Just Natalya's and Austin's prints where you would expect from the people living in the house, except no prints at all on obvious surfaces like doorknobs and faucets."

"Again, if Austin killed Natalya, why would he bother to wipe his prints from the doorknobs or faucets?"

"Exactly." Damon pointed his finger at her. "Did

you eat lunch? I have a half a sandwich left over. I'm supposed to be on a diet. Even though my girlfriend's not here, I can hear her voice in my head telling me not to eat the rest of that sandwich."

"She's watching you." Jane glanced at the picture of the pretty woman in beaded braids, assuming she was Damon's girlfriend. "I can probably eat it later. Still have the smell of the morgue in my nostrils."

Damon tipped down the picture of him and his girlfriend. Then he picked up the bag and dropped it on her desk. "Take it. Now I really don't feel like eating."

Jane picked up the bag with two fingers and moved it, revealing a message beneath. She held it up. "Did you take this?"

"I must've been at lunch. I didn't even see it on your desk. Is it about the case?"

"Not sure." She turned the pink slip of paper over. "Just a phone number with a message to call back. Looks like Billy's handwriting."

"Detective Crouch left about an hour ago."

Jane shoved back from her desk and returned the call on her work cell. She held it away from her ear when a machine-generated greeting started its spiel. "Not very helpful."

She left her name and number and delved into her email, looking for Dr. Ellis's report.

Several hours later, after Damon had left for the day, Jane stretched and gathered her files. As she stuffed her laptop into her bag, her mind strayed to Tim. She had an urge to call and tell him about the bruise and needle mark on Natalya's arm. She gripped her phone hard. He hadn't told her about Austin's connection to Russia.

When her phone buzzed in her hand, she almost dropped it. Had she conjured Tim just by thinking about him?

Then she glanced at the display and the unknown number she'd called earlier. She answered. "Detective Falco."

A man's voice rasped over the line. "Are you the cop in charge of the investigation into the murder of Natalya Petrova?"

Her fingertips buzzed. "Yes. Who are you? Do you have information?"

"This is Austin Walker, and I just wanna say, I didn't do it."

Her pulse ticked up several notches. "Where are you, Austin?"

"If I tell you, you can't come in with guns blazing. I didn't do it. I can't be arrested. Do you understand? I can't be arrested. They'll kill me."

"Who?"

"I can prove my innocence and point you in the right direction, but you have to meet me—alone. No cop cars, no lights. I'll run and you'll never hear from me again."

Jane scooped in a long breath. This was the kind of connection that solved cases. "Where are you?"

"You'll come alone? I'll be able to tell, and if I see anything, I'm running."

"I'll come alone. When and where?"

"Griffith Park. Near the train. What do you look like? What are you going to be wearing?"

"I'm tall. I have brown hair. I'm wearing a dark blue suit with a white blouse. You're not going to see any women in the park with a suit on at this time of night, or any time of night. I'll be alone, but I'll have my weapon. If you try anything, I'll shoot you."

"Fair enough. Can you be here in an hour?"

"How do I know you're really Austin Walker?"

"My real name is Oleg Stepanchikov. An American family adopted me from an orphanage in Russia when I was ten years old, and I changed my name. Oh, and Natalya has a tattoo of a Matryoshka doll on her upper thigh." He ended on a sob that sounded real enough.

"One hour."

It would take her less than an hour to get to Griffith Park, and she didn't want to spook the guy. She dropped her bag on her desk and dug into Damon's soggy left-over sandwich.

Almost an hour later, she cruised into the parking lot closest to the train ride at the empty park. When she exited her vehicle, she pulled out her gun and kept it at her side. She didn't want to scare off Austin, but she didn't want him to ambush her either.

Her boots crunched against the dirt as she approached the silent train. She called out. "Austin?"

The bushes behind her rustled and she whipped her head around, flicking on her flashlight. "Austin?"

Her nostrils twitched and her adrenaline pumped as she caught a whiff of gunpowder in the air. "Austin?"

She strode toward the bushes, her light scanning the area. She stumbled to a stop when her beam picked up a pair of white tennis shoes protruding from the underbrush.

As she crept closer, she illuminated the rest of Austin's body—flat on his back, a red puddle blooming from his partially blown away head.

She gripped her weapon in front of her and shouted. "Come out of the bushes now, or I'm shooting."

The branches of a tree parted, and Tim stepped into her light, hands up. "This is the second time you've had me at gunpoint in two days."

Chapter Four

Tim's muscles tensed as he watched Jane's eyes narrow and glitter in the darkness. One wrong move and he wouldn't put it past her to pump a bullet into his chest. That was what he liked about her—her commitment to a cause.

She stepped back and holstered her weapon. Barely above a whisper, she said, "Did you kill him?"

"Of course not." He spread his arms, splaying his fingers to show her he didn't have a gun.

"What are you doing here? How did you know Austin was meeting me in Griffith Park?" She folded her arms over her chest, her long fingers bunching into the fabric of her suit jacket.

"Was he?" He shuffled his feet away from Austin's blood soaking into the dirt. "Why would you be meeting a murder suspect in the park, at night, alone?"

"I'm a cop." She spat out the words.

He peered around her shoulder. "Do you have backup?"

Her fingers curled into tight fists, until he thought she'd rip the material with her bare hands. "I'm asking the questions. What are you doing here? Who killed Austin?"

"I don't know who killed Austin." Although he had some ideas. "He was dead when I got here."

"And why *are* you here? You lied to me about Austin Walker, although I don't know why that should surprise me." She dipped her hand into her pants pocket and pulled out a phone. "I'm calling this in. You can explain while we wait."

As she got on her cell, Tim crouched next to the dead body. Single gunshot to the back of the head, execution style. Did Austin even know it was coming? What did he have for Jane?

He glanced up at her, still on the phone, her back to him. He reached into the pockets of Austin's hoodie and pinched a piece of paper between his fingers. He studied the receipt by the light of his phone, and then stuffed it back inside the hoodie.

With his eyes on Jane, he slipped his fingers into the front pockets of Austin's jeans, tracing the outline of his key fob. He patted Austin's back pocket and pulled out a thin wallet. As Jane turned to face him, he dropped the wallet into the pocket of his jacket. The cops didn't need the wallet to ID Austin. Jane could verify she was meeting him, and they could get his prints.

She aimed her flashlight at Austin's body, the beam playing over the dead man's face. "Does he have his phone?"

"The phone is gone, along with his wallet—as if we'd believe this was a common robbery." He snorted for effect.

"Are you going to tell me what you were doing here? You must've been following Austin, or he planned a meeting with you, too." She scuffed the toe of her boot into the dirt, inches from Austin's hand. "If you knew where he was and you were following him, why didn't you tell me last night? He was my prime suspect."

"Was?" Tim lifted his eyebrows. "He's not still?"

Jabbing a finger at the ground, she said, "Does he look like a prime suspect to you? That's not a suicide, unless he's a contortionist and was able to get his arm around his back and then throw the gun somewhere before he died. Do you see a gun anywhere?"

A siren wailed in the distance, and Tim pushed himself up from the ground, brushing his hands together. "That's my signal to *vamanos*. I'll answer questions at your place, later. Meet me there."

She glanced over her shoulder at the approaching red and blue revolving lights. "And I'm supposed to pretend you were never here?"

"Tell them what you like. I'm not answering their questions." He slipped back through the trees and clambered up the trail to his car. He'd give Jane a few answers, but he'd have to stay a couple of steps ahead of her. His mentor, James, warned him never to give anything away. Same code as the biker gang his father ran.

He didn't care if she told the others that she'd found him with Austin's body when she arrived. She knew he didn't kill Austin, and she'd have to start answering some questions of her own about his presence. Jane didn't want to be in that position. By protecting him, she'd be protecting herself.

Tim slid into his car and released his parking brake. After he rolled down the hill several feet, he punched on his engine and killed the lights. When he hit the main road out of the park, he turned his headlights back on and cruised to the freeway.

Jane wouldn't be finished with that scene for another few hours, and he had a wallet to check out.

ABOUT TWO HOURS LATER, Jane's car pulled into her driveway. Tim hadn't tried to hide his presence this time and flicked his lights at her before he maneuvered his way out of his vehicle, a bottle of wine under one arm and a pie balancing on his hand.

She slammed her car door and put a fist on her hip. "If you think those gifts are going to get you out of answering some questions, you're delusional."

"No delusions." He gripped the bottle by its neck and raised it. "Just noticed that the bottle you had last night was down to the dregs, and I figured it had probably been a while since you had dinner and might want some dessert. Fresh-baked from the diner where I had my coffee while waiting for you. It is missing one piece."

She spun around without a thank-you, the heels of her boots crunching on the gravel of her driveway. She'd kept the rustic look of the house by avoiding cement and allowing the foliage from the canyon to creep onto her property. Isolated but pretty.

He knew this setting used to host upscale parties, and twinkling lights had been strung in the trees to welcome well-heeled guests. But the parties and entertainment had stopped when Jane had divorced her husband—after he punched her in the mouth.

She turned to him when she reached the porch. "I kept your name out of it, but that doesn't mean I'm letting you off the hook…and we found the gun."

Tim almost dropped the pie as he stumbled after her into the house. "You're kidding. Where was it?"

"It was under Austin's body. If we'd rolled him over, we would've seen it." She tossed her purse on a table in the entryway and dropped her keys into an artistic-looking tray that probably cost a bundle.

He said, "Doesn't sound like you're convinced it's a suicide, even with the gun at the scene."

She shrugged out of her jacket and sat on an ottoman to remove her boots.

Tim swallowed as he watched her. How much more was she going to take off? She'd removed her shoes the last time he was here, but had kept the jacket—armor to ward him off. Was she beginning to shed her armor, let him in?

"Suicide is too convenient." With her shoes off, she wiggled her toes.

Tim dragged his gaze away from the strangely erotic sight. "I'm going to open this wine and pour us both a glass. Pie?"

"I thought you didn't like wine, and I don't have any ice cream." She straightened to her full height and sauntered into the kitchen, brushing past him. She retrieved two wineglasses from the cupboard and put them on the counter. Tapping a drawer, she said, "Corkscrew."

"I need the fortification for the third degree you're

gonna give me, and I know you don't stock beer." He flipped open the lid of the pie box. "We don't need ice cream. It's a banana cream pie."

"Mmm." She reached past him to grab a plate, her breast skimming his arm.

Maybe *she* was trying to get on *his* good side. He didn't even care. He preferred this version of Jane to last night's prickly one.

He pulled the cork from the bottle with a dull pop and filled the glasses halfway. As he handed the ruby red liquid to her, he said, "Let the interrogation commence."

"Commence? You're beginning to sound like a Fibbie, Ruskin. Did they finally get to you? Is the pocket protector next?" She clinked her glass with his. "Let's take this out to the deck."

He followed on her heels like an eager puppy, mesmerized by her swaying hips. If she kept this up, he just might tell her everything.

She opened the French doors onto a deck that overlooked the canyon. It afforded the same view as the one from the window, but outside the sounds and smells of the canyon enveloped you, permeating your senses.

Tim took a deep breath before taking a long pull of his wine. This setting and Jane's company almost made him forget they'd just come from the brutal slaying of a young man. He eased into the Adirondack chair beside her, cupping his glass. "What do you want to know?"

"I want to know why you were at Griffith Park. How did you know Austin would be there?" She wedged her bare feet against the wood railing.

"We had a tracker on his phone. Could follow him whether or not the phone was turned on." He stole a sideways glance at her. "We were keeping tabs on him—even before Natalya was murdered."

"So you must've known Austin wasn't responsible for her murder. You would've been able to tell from his phone's location that he wasn't in the house at the time—unless he was."

He lifted his shoulders. "I'd have to know the time of death. He was at the house. He could've been responsible."

"Why were you following Austin before the murder of his girlfriend?"

He turned and sipped from his glass, his eyes meeting hers over the rim. "Russian mob."

"Austin Walker. That…kid was in the Bratva here in LA?"

"You know he was adopted from Russia, right?"

She nodded. "Oleg Stepanchikov. Came here from a Russian orphanage when he was ten."

"Stepanchikov is quite the name in Russia. His bio father was what we'd call a boss or capo here. When he started singing, the mob murdered Austin's whole family in Moscow. The government there wanted to get him out of the country as soon as possible and American adoptions of Russian children were big at the time." An owl hooted in the distance, and Tim swirled his wine. "But some people never forget."

Jane dropped her feet to the deck and hunched forward. "What are you telling me? Austin was in the mob because of his father, sort of a legacy member, or you were watching him because others were watching him?"

"Not absolutely sure. I don't think he was involved in any criminal activity—yet."

"What does it have to do with poor Natalya?" She rubbed a smudge of lipstick from the rim of her glass with her thumb.

"Not sure about that yet, either."

"Obviously, Austin didn't kill her. Her death must have something to do with Austin's involvement with the Russian mob. Maybe the rival gang discovered his identity here in the US and came after him to finish the job. Natalya got in the way."

"Could just be a simple domestic. Kid like that, with his background?" He rolled his shoulders. "Lotta anger there."

"From the little you told me, there was a lotta anger in your background, too, but you didn't murder anyone."

One of Tim's hands clenched the arm of the chair. "Came close a few times."

"So did I." Jane's fingers hovered at her wine-stained lips.

"Some people deserve it." He clasped his hands between his knees. If he'd been present when Jane's ex had punched her, he'd have gone ballistic. But all that had happened before he and Jane met, when she was still on shaky ground.

"Some people, but not Natalya." She propped her chin in her hand. "Unless you're going to tell me Natalya was involved with the Russian mob, too."

"Maybe in a peripheral way—but as the exploited, not the exploiter."

Jane flattened her hand against her stomach. "Do you mean she was in danger of being trafficked?"

"We don't know for sure. You're probably aware that the Russian mob is big on human trafficking." Tim clenched his jaw, recalling the empty warehouse.

"That's even more reason to believe Austin didn't kill Natalya in a crime of passion. Maybe she was making a run for it, or threatened to go to the police."

Tim held up one finger. "Or Austin was there to spy on Natalya and keep her in line. When she stepped out of that line, he took action and did kill her. We just don't know at this point."

"We would've known a lot more if I had gotten a chance to talk to Austin. I don't believe for one minute he offed himself."

Tim asked, "Did he say what he wanted to talk to you about and why he couldn't just tell you over the phone? I know he called you from a burner phone because he'd turned his off. Why couldn't he just give you the goods over the phone?"

Jane's eyelashes fluttered, and she took a long pull from her wineglass. "I'm not sure. I asked and he didn't answer. He insisted that we meet."

If he saw that reaction interrogating a suspect, he'd order a polygraph in no time flat. He took a long breath through his nose, the pine scent from the canyon clearing his sinuses. He needed some clarity.

"What did he tell you?"

"Not much." Jane sealed her lips. "What did you see when you got to the park?"

"Austin's dead body."

"Did you smell gunpowder? Did you hear anything? See anything?"

"He was dead when I got there, and his killer was long gone. I did a quick search of the area, and didn't find a thing. There were no cars where I parked, so I'm thinking whoever killed him parked on your side. Or he hiked in, concealing his car."

Jane scooted forward in her chair and pushed up to her feet. She crossed her arms on the railing and gazed into the canyon. "At least we have the gun and the bullet. We're going to trace it. We're getting Austin's phone records, and we'll look at his past texts and calls. We'll get to the bottom of it."

"I have no doubt you'll do your best. You're a good detective, Jane. We never would've solved that other case without you." He stood beside her, his shoulder bumping hers. "And for the record, the time we spent together was not a chore for me. Hell, I would've been with you even if I weren't trying to get information about the case. You gotta know that, right?"

She braced her forearms against the railing and rolled her head to the side, her loose hair falling over her face. "I think I do. What we had was too…real."

His heart stuttered in his chest. This was the first time she'd acknowledged that his feelings hadn't just been about his undercover work.

He took one of her hands, and laced his fingers through hers. "It was more real than anything I'd ever felt in my life. Hurting you was the last thing I wanted to do. I was trying to figure out a way I could extricate myself from the job and reenter your life as my real self. Give us a chance to start over."

Her mouth curled up at one corner. "I always wondered how much different you were in real life from Terry Rush, your alter ego."

Brushing a lock of hair from her cheek and tucking it behind her ear, he said, "One thing old Terry and I had in common was that we were both crazy about you."

She turned toward him, her lips parted, her eyes wide.

It must've been the magic of the night, but he'd take it before something reminded Jane how much she'd hated him when she discovered he'd been undercover and had engineered a meeting with her to find out what she knew about a drug trafficking case she'd been working.

With a slight tremble, he slid his hand through her hair to cup the back of her head. He pulled her toward him, and her arms went around his waist as if they belonged there.

Their lips met and the dark berry and honey hints from the wine mingled in their kiss.

She nibbled his lower lip as her hands slipped lower, skimming across his backside. Her need for him made him hard, and he deepened the kiss, melding his chest against her soft breasts.

Her hands hovered at his belt, and she edged her fingertips into the top of his front pockets, urging him closer. In her bare feet, Jane was maybe an inch or two shorter than he was, and Tim shifted to fit his pelvis against hers for maximum connection.

All at once, Jane shoved her fingers into his pocket and planted her palm on his chest. As she snatched her hand from his pocket, she shoved him with the other hand.

Stumbling back, he blinked, as if coming out of a daydream. When he could focus, he saw Jane waving a key in his face.

"Is this what you took off Austin's dead body?"

Chapter Five

Jane's lips, still throbbing from Tim's kiss, spread into a smile—or the approximation of one. Tricking Tim hadn't given her the pleasure she'd expected.

His handsome face creased in confusion as he patted the pocket she'd just pilfered. "What?"

She pinched the key between her fingers, and it winked in the low light of the deck, as if in on the joke. "I saw you taking something from Austin's body when I turned to call for backup. I knew if I asked you about it, you'd just come up with more lies. So I waited for an opportunity and took it off you."

Shaking his head, he ran a hand over his mouth. "I see what you did there. Very sneaky."

"Sometimes you have to fight fire with fire." She closed her fist around the key. "You snagged this a few hours ago. What have you found out about it? Don't tell me you spent all your time shopping for wine and a banana cream pie."

Tim sat back in his chair and crossed his hands behind his head, gradually reclaiming his self-assuredness.

She'd caught him off guard for a second or two, but he'd shrugged it off like a pro.

"I took his wallet, and I found the key there. I don't know what it is." He braced a foot against the railing. "Do you?"

She perched on the arm of the chair. "Why would I know, and why would I tell you if I did?"

"You went there to meet Austin for a reason. He couldn't tell you what he wanted over the phone, so it makes sense that he had to give you something in person. That might be the key."

"He didn't tell me anything else over the phone, just insisted that we meet in person." She rubbed her chin. "Whoever shot him took his phone, unless you have that, too. Maybe his killer took whatever else Austin was going to give me."

"I don't have the phone. Austin had tucked the key in his wallet, hidden away. The killer could've heard me coming and had only enough time to grab the phone." Tim stretched his arms to the sky. "C'mon, Jane. If you'd have found that key, you wouldn't have told me, either."

She drilled a finger into her chest. "That's because it's my investigation. This case belongs to the LAPD, not the FBI."

"Because it involves Natalya and Austin, it belongs to us, too. We've been tracking this Russian gang's activities in LA for a long time. We've made a few arrests, but we've never gotten to the top. We've never been able to put a stop to their various rackets—drugs, weapons…and girls." Tim clenched his fists and pounded the arms of the chair. "If you could see what they did to these young women."

"I saw what they did to Natalya." She tipped her head to the side and slid from the arm into the seat of the chair, her legs hanging over the side. "Why does this one have you all wound up?"

He flexed his hands. "We were so close a few weeks ago. We had a line on a warehouse in San Pedro. We saw the evidence that they'd held people there in cages...*in cages*. We staked it out, but we were too late. I think someone tipped them off."

"You think that someone is in the LAPD?" Jane swung her legs back and forth over the arm of the chair. It was not as if she couldn't believe that, but why did he have to include her in his suspicions?

Tim dropped his chin to his chest. "Could be."

"Is that why you hid the key from me?" Her toes crept up to the arm of his chair, inches from his hand.

"It's not that I don't trust you, Jane, but you do work for the LAPD. You'd have to log evidence from the crime scene. Anyone could see your report."

"You couldn't just come to me and let me know?" She puffed out a breath. "I can tell you right now that the prevailing belief in the department is that Austin killed Natalya in a domestic and then offed himself."

"Tossing his phone in the process? Why'd he call you?"

She lifted her shoulders. "To find his body?"

"Or, to give you the key."

Cupping the key in the palm of her hand, she asked, "What do you think it is?"

"I examined it closely—in between getting the pie and wine. There are some numbers stamped on it, but I think those are meaningless. It's too big for a padlock, too small for a door key."

"Depends on the door." She held up the key between her thumb and forefinger. "You mentioned a warehouse in San Pedro. This could fit a lock in one of those roll-up metal doors on a warehouse or storage unit."

"All we need to do is try it on about a thousand of those throughout LA." He clamped a hand on the back of his neck and twisted his head from side to side.

"We don't have Austin's physical phone, but that doesn't mean we can't get a record of his activity, including the GPS. In fact, didn't you tell me earlier that the FBI was tracking his phone? That's how you followed him to Griffith Park, right?"

"I checked. The tracker went dead. Either his killer destroyed the phone when he took it or located and disabled the tracking device. They took the burner, too."

Jane said, "We can still probably track his movements using his cell, at least his movements prior to his murder if his phone has been destroyed."

Tim snapped his fingers. "See if he's been to San Pedro, or Long Beach, for that matter. We always did work well together, Jane."

"If you really believed that, you wouldn't have tried to shut me out." She held up her hand and ticked off her fingers. "You knew where Austin was all along. You followed him. You took something from his body without telling me. That's not working together."

With his warm palm, he rubbed the top of her foot,

still parked on the arm of his chair. "I trust you, Jane. I don't trust your department."

"That's funny, because most of the department feels the same way about the FBI." She slid her foot from beneath his hand. She couldn't argue with Tim when his touch sent chills through her body.

He worried a thumbnail with his teeth. "Are you going to put the key in your report?"

"If you have reason to believe the investigation could be compromised, I'll think twice about it." The department thought she had an open-and-shut case here—murder and then suicide. If everyone else backed off the investigation, she could be free to do some work on her own. She'd have to include Damon, though. She could trust Damon and wanted to build on the relationship they were growing. She needed a solid partner by her side—one who didn't do funny things to her insides.

Tim's low voice rumbled beside her. "I didn't even mind that you used me to get the key. Gave me hope there for a minute. Some things can't be faked."

Grateful for the low lights, Jane turned her warm face away from Tim. "I'm sorry, but I couldn't think of any other way to get it. But why did I have to resort to that?"

"You know I don't trust easily, Jane. Never had much of a reason to trust anyone in my life."

Her nose tingled. "And I do? I thought I'd found my Prince Charming in Aaron."

"You did, and then he changed." He drummed his fingers on the chair. "People can change for the worse as well as the better."

"But did he change, or did I just miss the signs at the beginning of the relationship? Maybe he always had that violence in him and instead of recognizing it and staying clear, I recognized it and gravitated toward him because of it." She spread her hands. "You know what they say—you duplicate the relationships you know, and that's the kind of relationship my parents had."

He grabbed her hand and threaded his fingers through hers. "You do that until you realize you're doing it, and then you start making better choices."

"Are you making better choices?" She left her hand in his. "Or are you still coming to the rescue of women who need your help?"

Did Lana count? "I didn't think you needed my help—at least not at first."

"That was different. You needed *my* help…and that was work related." She disentangled her fingers from his and pushed up from the chair. "I'm going to try that pie."

He murmured beside her in the dark. "It wasn't just work related."

"Do you want more pie? I'm going on my laptop to see if I can discover anything more about the key." She jerked her thumb over her shoulder at the house.

"Might as well get started." He collected both of their wineglasses from the deck with one hand. "I do have an idea about the key that I don't mind sharing with you."

"That's a first." She stepped into the house and flipped open her laptop, which was charging on the kitchen island. "Yes or no on the dessert?"

"I'll take another piece if you have some coffee I can brew."

"Are you kidding?" She glanced over her shoulder from the open fridge. "I still have that contraption in the corner that can make coffee, steam milk and probably do your taxes for you."

"But do you still have coffee for it?"

"I occasionally crank it up and even grind the beans." She tapped the cupboard above the coffee machine. "There's some already ground in there."

As Tim puttered with the coffee, she cut two slices from the pie and licked the cream from her fingers. She slid her plate next to the laptop and fished the key from her pocket. She brought up images of different keys as she held up the real thing next to the screen. "I think this might take ten years."

Tim straddled the stool next to her and dug into his pie. "We can rule out some of these. It's not a key to a safe-deposit box. It's not a house or apartment key."

"Too small for a mailbox key." She squinted at the screen.

He hunched forward, a little bit of cream from the pie clinging to his chin. "Bring up some storage units or warehouses."

Her gaze flicked away from his chin, and she reached for the paper towel roll. She yanked off half a piece and waved it in his face. "You have food on your face."

"There goes my suave persona." He dragged the paper towel across his face.

"Okay, storage unit keys." She scanned the images on the monitor. "Could be. It's about the right size. You said you had another idea while we wait for Austin's phone records."

"Coffee?" He slid from the stool and held up a mug he'd taken from her cupboard.

"No, thanks. If you want to use the steamer thing, I have milk."

"This was complicated enough. I'll drink it black."

A minute later, he settled beside her again, the steam rising from his cup and the dark, rich smell of the coffee making her think of lazy Sunday mornings.

Putting the key between them on the counter, she asked, "Your idea?"

"I already know where one of their warehouses is in San Pedro." He nudged the key with his finger. "We could try this one out there. It's not the exact key but if it fits the locks in that facility, we'll know the unit is in the general area, or at least that it's a similar unit."

"Are these warehouses or storage units?"

"There's a combination of both. Some storage containers, small warehouses and some bigger ones that belong to shipping companies and exporters, depending on what side of the docks they're on. That particular place has a mixture of all sorts."

"Sounds good." She stuffed a huge forkful of pie into her mouth and closed out of the browser on her laptop. Then she hopped off the stool.

Tim's dark eyes widened. "You mean now?"

"If I had time to waste, I'd wait for Austin's phone records. How do we know this gang isn't targeting other young women in the area?"

"I'm sure they are." Tim's jaw tightened. "That's what they do. That's what we've been investigating."

"Then why are we sitting here eating banana cream pie?"

Tim took a gulp of his coffee, and then waved his hand in front of his mouth. "Because I remembered it was your favorite... I remember a lot of your favorite things."

Jane almost tripped on her way to grabbing her jacket off the back of the chair. Then she set her jaw.

They could work together, but she'd be damned if she'd let Tim Ruskin in her bed again. He was already taking up too much space in her heart.

TIM SWALLOWED THE bitterness rising from his throat as he wheeled the car into the parking lot next to one of San Pedro's docks. They'd been so close last time—so close to rescuing those women and making their captors pay. So close to finding Lana—or at least some information about her.

Jane exhaled a long breath. "This is where they were keeping the women?"

"For a while, anyway." He tapped on the inside of the window. "An international port gives them plenty of opportunities to ship the women overseas."

"In containers?" Jane placed her long fingers against her throat.

"That's what we're dealing with, Jane. Are you sure you're in?"

She unclipped her seat belt and allowed it to retract

with a crack. "I'm a cop, Tim. You seem to forget that sometimes."

He snorted. "As if you'd ever allow that."

She'd been working even as she'd wrapped her arms around his waist and touched her lips to his. He didn't mind. He'd take her any way he could get her.

She tapped the side of his head with her finger. "Where to?"

"Sorry." He eased his foot from the brake, and the car rolled forward. The rows of grubby, silver warehouses looked the same, so he counted back from the water's edge to the location of the warehouse they'd raided earlier.

They'd never allowed Octavio Galindo to clean the space that night. Instead, they'd brought him in for questioning. The man had never seen the person who hired him. It had all been arranged online, and their tech people hadn't been able to trace the IP address of Galindo's contact.

They'd processed the warehouse, but hadn't come up with much evidence—nothing that could be traced, anyway.

He rolled to a stop and shifted into Park in front of the squat metal building that had once caged the futures and dreams of several young women. Where were they now? Was Lana among them?

He nodded once. "That's it."

"Let's give it a try." Jane cracked open her door. "Can you leave your headlights on, or should we use flashlights instead?"

"I don't want to draw attention to our presence here. Let's go with the flashlights."

Jane reached into the back seat for her bag. "I don't see how there can be much security if they missed a human trafficking deal right beneath their noses."

"There are a lot of buildings here. That and the proximity to the water make this a perfect spot."

"Except we're here now." Jane dug in her bag and pulled out a flashlight. She didn't have a gun in there. She was already strapped, but Tim's eyebrows shot up when she withdrew a knife from the bag.

"You never know." She shrugged and rolled up the pant leg of her jeans and tucked the knife into a sheath around her calf.

"Remind me never to mess with you."

"Didn't stop you before." She clambered from the car and he cringed, expecting her to slam the door, but she eased it closed with a click.

He followed her out of the car as she shined a path with her flashlight. She still had Austin's key. She'd probably never give it up to him now.

He stepped in front of her, nudging her with his shoulder. "Let me."

Her gaze dropped to his outstretched hand, and she dropped the key in his palm. "You don't think there's anyone in there now, do you?"

"I wish, but I'm sure they haven't been back since they cleared the women out. We were expecting them to show up the night of our stakeout and collect the cages they'd left behind. Erase their dirty deeds, but all we got was the guy they'd hired to clean up for them."

He pinched the key between his fingers and fitted it into the lock, the harsh sound of metal scraping against metal louder than it should be.

He tried to turn the key, but it stopped, as he'd expected it to.

Jane grabbed his wrist. "The key fits. There must be another warehouse here that it unlocks."

Stepping back, Tim glanced down the row of identical warehouses. "It might not even be in this block."

"Maybe not, but there has to be some kind of port authority here that rents out these warehouses to businesses. They should be able to tell us which one this key belongs to."

"I hope so." A shuffling sound had Tim holding up his hand. "Shh."

Jane froze, shifting her gaze to the side and reaching for her weapon.

She'd heard it, too.

Tim pocketed the key and ducked into a crouch. At the same moment, someone fired a shot and the bullet clanged against the metal above his head, making his ears ring.

"Get down, Jane!"

She slid down beside him and lunged for the car, stationing herself behind the engine block, bracing her weapon on the hood. "LAPD! Stop!"

Another bullet hit the passenger window, and footsteps pounded against the asphalt.

Jane popped up from behind the car and squeezed off a shot. "He's getting away. The water."

Tim peeled himself from the gritty ground and sprang

to his feet. He gave chase, zigzagging, making himself a more difficult target to hit.

The sound of an outboard motor cut through the night, jangling his nerves even more. Tim charged toward it, Jane barking orders behind him. As a bullet whizzed by his head, too close for comfort, Tim took the only cover afforded to him…and dove headfirst into the water.

Chapter Six

Panic surged through Jane's body as she watched Tim fall forward and disappear into the darkness. The engine of some kind of boat died away as it sped away from the dock.

Keeping her weapon pointed in front of her, Jane jogged toward the water's edge. "Tim! Tim!"

Splashing noises greeted her, and she coiled her muscles, ready to drop her gun and jump in to save Tim. She aimed her flashlight into the murky water, and a figure broke the surface. She pointed her gun in the same direction as the beam of light.

Tim shouted, his arms raised. "Would you stop pointing weapons at me?"

Jane's knees finally gave, and she sank to the asphalt at the edge of the dock. "Are you okay? Did he hit you?"

With his head bobbing above the water, Tim breast-stroked to the side. "I dove under the water to avoid the gunfire. He got away in a small dinghy. They must have another boat in the area. They're not taking that thing out on the open water."

"There was more than one person?" Jane holstered her gun with shaky hands.

"One guy with a gun, shooting at us, and another guy driving the getaway boat." He hoisted himself from the water, streams of it sluicing from his body.

Jane eyed his shirt, plastered to his chest. "You're a mess."

"Give me a minute." He rolled onto his back, panting, digging his thumb and forefinger into his eyes. "They're watching this place for some reason."

"It can't be because they're trying to see who knows about their warehouse." She crouched beside him, the water from his clothes running toward her shoes. "You guys already made the warehouse, already searched it."

Tim hitched up on his elbows. "You'd think they'd be watching the warehouse that belongs to Austin's key instead of this one, which is played out."

Jane fell back on her bottom, drawing her knees to her chest and wrapping her arms around her legs. She folded her hands to keep them from sweeping a lock of wet, dark hair from Tim's eyes. "Maybe they don't know about the other warehouse...if there is one. They could suspect, just like us, and that's why they're watching. The person who killed Austin took his phone, probably looking for how much and what he knew. He was obviously killed to prevent him from talking to me—or anyone else."

"They set him up for the murder to keep him away from the cops." Tim hunched his shoulders, and his teeth chattered.

"Why are we sitting here with you soaking wet?"

Jane struggled to her feet and stretched out a hand to Tim. "You're sure you're okay?"

"Fine." He clasped her hand and allowed her to pull him up. "But it's getting cold out here."

"Especially if you're drenched." She chafed his chilled hand with both of hers. "Come back to my place, and I'll toss your stuff in the dryer and get you something hot to drink."

"That sounds good." He clenched his jaw and wrung out his shirt. "Maybe you can talk to the leasing agent of this place tomorrow and find out where that key belongs."

"I'll give that a try. Despite what happened, I'm not sorry we came." Jane faced the water, narrowing her eyes. "Austin knew something and the person or people who killed Natalya are desperate to keep us in the dark."

By the time Tim pulled into her driveway, behind her car, he'd stopped shivering. He turned to her. "I can make it back to my hotel without succumbing to hypothermia. It's getting late."

"Don't put on the brave face. Your teeth stopped chattering just about fifteen minutes ago. Besides, you have to help me finish that pie. You're not leaving that with me. I'll keep the wine."

"Deal." He cut the engine and squished out of the car, leaving rivulets of water behind him.

When they reached the doorway, Tim toed off his wet running shoes and picked them up by the laces. "Can you toss these in the dryer, too?"

"Yeah, but you probably don't want to leave them in too long. You can drive home in socks." She crossed through the kitchen to the laundry room and pulled open the door to the dryer. "In here."

Standing in the middle of her kitchen, he peeled the wet shirt over his head. "I'd strip to my skivvies, but they're wet, too. They gotta join the other clothes."

Jane spun around, holding her finger in the air. "My brother left some things here the last time he blew through LA. I think I can find a pair of running shorts or sweats and a T-shirt for you."

He cocked his head, bunching his damp shirt in front of him. "Isn't your brother about six foot nine?"

"He wishes. If he'd been six-nine instead of six-four, maybe he would've made it in the NBA instead of peaking in college."

"They still called him Falco the Falcon, and he has about five inches on me."

"The sweats might be a little long, but Falco the Falcon had nothing on you in the muscle department." Her cheeks heated as her gaze flicked across Tim's chiseled chest. Did she just say that? *Muscle department?*

She dipped her head and squeezed past him. "I'll get those clothes."

When she got to the guest bedroom, Jane leaned against the wall, closed her eyes and took a deep breath. She needed to get a grip here. When Tim had disappeared from her line of sight at the same time she heard gunfire, a black cloud had swept through her at the thought of losing him. She didn't have to make up for that now. He was fine...and he was the same old FBI agent playing fast and loose with the truth and keeping information from her. Nothing had changed—even if he was almost naked in her laundry room.

She pushed off the wall and yanked open the closet door, folding it back. Her brother, Johnny, had played some professional ball in Italy and had stayed there to coach. He usually crashed with her when he wound up in the States and had left a collection of clothes here in the past few years.

She snagged a T-shirt from a hanger and dug through a basket of clean clothes on the closet floor, dragging out a pair of dark blue sweats.

She draped the items over her arm and returned to the kitchen, not sure what she would find. She peeked into the laundry room.

Tim turned from stuffing his clothes in the dryer. A pair of wet boxers hung low on his flat waist, clinging to his muscled thighs and outlining…everything else.

He flashed his teeth. "You're right. It feels good to get out of those wet clothes."

She thrust out the shirt and sweats. "You can wear these until your clothes dry. Do you want to take a shower, too? I can't imagine that water was very clean."

He twisted his head to the side and sniffed his arm. "Smells like diesel. I'll take that shower."

She backed out of the kitchen, giving him privacy to remove the last of his clothing. She'd seen his naked body before, of course, but they didn't need to go there tonight.

She left him to his own devices, as he knew where the guest bathroom was located and where she kept the towels.

They'd spent many idyllic evenings in this house,

exploring each other, mind and body—until she'd discovered she didn't know him at all.

She slammed her bedroom door shut and stepped out of her jeans. She pulled on a pair of flannel pajama bottoms and swapped out her shirt, grimy from the dock, for a loose-fitting, white cotton tank top, tossing aside the lacy camisole she usually wore to bed. She didn't want to give Tim any ideas—it was bad enough *she* had those ideas.

She perched on the edge of her bed, listening to the shower downstairs, trying not to imagine Tim in it. She'd tried to put memories of him behind her and as long as he was out of sight, those feelings were out of mind. Being in his presence caused all those old feelings to bubble to the surface. All it had taken was one punch from her ex to end that marriage, and just one betrayal from Tim to end that relationship—not that she equated Aaron's violence with Tim declining to tell her he was an undercover FBI agent. But after Aaron, she didn't allow anyone to play her for a fool.

The shower ended and still she waited. She didn't want to take any chances of walking in on Tim in the buff. The man had very little modesty when it came to his body. Why should he? He had muscles to spare on a tight frame. She didn't even mind that she could best him by a few inches in four-inch heels. He carried himself with so much confidence he seemed seven feet tall to her.

She took a deep breath, bounded from the bed and jogged down the stairs. He'd better be fully dressed this time.

"I thought maybe you'd gone to sleep on me."

Given the direction of her previous thoughts, she felt the heat in her cheeks. "Had a few things to do upstairs."

Tim held the wine bottle aloft, dark hair slicked back. "Another glass?"

"Sure, but let's stay inside. It's getting chilly outside and you don't need any more cold seeping into your bones." She raised her eyebrows as she glanced at the sweats rolled up at the ankle. "Those fit okay?"

He pinched the T-shirt, pulling it away from his chest. "The shirt's okay, but your brother has some long legs."

"They go with his long arms." She floated past him and grabbed their used wineglasses from the kitchen counter. "You want another glass?"

"I'll take another." He patted his broad chest, drawing her attention to it again. "Might help me warm up inside."

"Are you still chilled?" She rinsed the glasses under the faucet, peering at the one with the lipstick imprint of her lips on the rim.

Rubbing his arm, he said, "A little."

She set the glasses down on the kitchen island with a clink and tapped the one on the right. "This one's yours."

"Then ladies first." He poured the dark, shimmering liquid into the glass on the left and handed it to her. He filled his own glass half-full and raised it. "To the best backup I've had in a long time."

She tapped her glass against his. "I couldn't offer much backup when you took off after the guy…in the dark. Is that what they teach you at the FBI Academy?"

"Some things can't be taught." He took a gulp of

wine, downing half of it. Rubbing his flat belly, he said, "Hit the spot."

She cupped her wineglass with one hand and sauntered to the couch. She positioned herself on one end, curling her leg beneath her. "We were obviously in the right spot. They weren't watching the warehouse you'd already searched. They were watching another place. Do you think they know which one Austin's key unlocks, or are they trying to find out?"

He sank into the recliner across from her, and she breathed a little easier at the distance between them. "If they knew which one was Austin's, they would've done something about it already—emptied it. Destroyed evidence, moved it. They suspect Austin knew something. That's why they killed him. I don't know why they think it had anything to do with the docks at San Pedro. Maybe they'd followed him there before."

"I think we should be able to find out where this key goes tomorrow. I'll contact the management company. They should be able to verify that it's a key to one of the containers or warehouses, and hopefully look up Austin in their records."

"Maybe we should've just waited until morning." Tim rubbed his knuckles across the dark, sexy stubble on his jaw. "Is that what they teach you at the LAPD Academy?"

"Some things you can't teach." She flicked her finger at her glass and took a sip. "You know, once I put this into the report it's going to be common knowledge at the station for anyone who cares to look."

"I know that." He pinched his chin. "Maybe it can be a way of smoking someone out."

"How do you know your mole or snitch isn't with your guys and not mine?"

"I don't really know anything for sure. Twice we had a line on the Bratva here in LA, sure things, and twice they thwarted us. Someone tipped them off. I'm sure of that." His jaw tightened.

She traced the rim of her glass with the tip of her finger. "You don't think it's one of your own undercover, tipping them off for the greater good, do you?"

His dark eyes locked onto hers. "Are you okay with that now? Seems like we had a lot of discussions about the greater good."

"Not when that greater good plays with people's emotions." She tossed back the rest of her wine and stood up too quickly. Her foot had fallen asleep, and she swayed to the side.

Tim shot up from his chair and grabbed her arm. "That's how you get on one glass? When did you turn into a lightweight?"

She glanced at the hand on her arm and ran her tongue along her bottom lip. She swayed again, this time toward Tim, unable to resist the magnetic pull he exerted over her.

Seemed he couldn't resist her any more than she could resist him. He curled an arm around her waist and pulled her close.

As he put his lips next to her ear, he whispered. "You got me all wrong."

She jerked back, all the reasons why she ended it between them rushing back. "I—I don't know, Tim. You got me at my lowest, after my divorce, after the cheating. I thought you were a shining light...and then I found out it was all a lie. Terry Rush was a lie."

Tim released her, and the emptiness flooded her again.

"I never lied about my feelings for you, Jane. While I might've drawn you in for the purposes of the case, that motive changed quickly. You're a great detective. Do you honestly believe you wouldn't have been able to see right through me?"

Dipping her head, she pressed her fingers against her temples. "I had no clue you were an undercover FBI agent. Do you know how that made me look to my fellow officers?"

"Is that what this is all about?" He flung his arms out to the side. "You're embarrassed because your ace detective skills couldn't sort out an undercover agent? I have skills, too, Jane."

He pounded his fist against his chest. "That wasn't my first undercover rodeo. My job is to fool everyone—even the local cops. My life depends on that."

"You could've told me." Her breath hitched in her throat as she swallowed a sob. "If the feelings were real, you could've told me."

"That's not how it works, and if we're talking about professional embarrassment here, how do you think it went over with my superiors when they found out I'd fallen for a detective working my case?"

"They didn't congratulate you on a job well done?"

"Hell no." He dragged a hand through his hair,

shorter now that he was no longer undercover. "I don't know what I can say or do to make you trust me."

Jane narrowed her eyes. "Tell me everything you know about this case and the gang that killed Natalya and now Austin."

"I think I've done that, Jane." He rubbed his eyes, and she knew he was lying.

The buzzer for the dryer sounded, and she stepped back. "Your clothes are dry."

He huffed out a breath and brushed past her. She almost reached for him, but he spun around and grabbed her. Wrapping his arms around her, he brought her to the floor. His body landed hard on the wood floor, and he positioned himself so that she fell on top of him, cushioning her fall.

Her mouth gaped open. Was there something inside her that attracted violent men? With her arms pinned against her body by Tim's vise-like grip, she couldn't move them. She struggled against him, yelling. "What is wrong with you? Get off me."

He released her and gasped as if the fall had knocked the breath from his lungs. "Stay down."

Shoving him with both hands, she coiled her legs beneath her to push up and away from him. "What are you talking about? You just tackled me. I'm not staying anywhere with you."

"Jane." He jerked his thumb toward the French doors to the deck. "I just saved your life."

Chapter Seven

Tim took another shuddering breath. His words had come out all wrong, and they failed to have the desired effect on Jane.

Her nostrils flared and her cheeks flushed. "That's your excuse for taking me down? Is this a joke?"

Pounding his chest with his fist, he coughed. "I mean it, Jane. There was a red beam on your forehead. Someone had a high-powered rifle aimed at you."

Her tawny-colored eyes popped as they shifted toward the doors to the deck and the canyon beyond. "A-are you kidding me?"

"You think I tackled you for the hell of it and made up a wild story to excuse my actions?" He grabbed her hands. "You know me better than that. Can you close those drapes?"

She had dropped back to the floor, her breathing heavy. "Of course I can close them. I just never do. There's nothing out there, Tim. The guy would have to be in a tree or a helicopter to aim a gun in here."

"I don't know how he did it but unless you want to spend the rest of the night on the floor—with me—

you'd better close those drapes." Not that the prospect of that didn't have its appeal.

"I'll do better than that." She army-crawled across the floor and wedged herself between the couch and a coffee table. Her hand felt along the surface of the table until her fingers curled around a remote control. "Watch this."

She pressed some buttons on the device, and solid blinds crept down over the glass doors to the canyon. Once the blinds settled in place, she pressed another control and a set of beige drapes slid across the closed blinds, meeting in the middle. Then the room went dark.

"Did you do that from the magical control, too, or did someone just cut the lights?"

"That was me." She held up the flat-surfaced remote sporting several buttons. "Aaron insisted on this thing. I could practically cook a meal from here with it."

"We may have to do that." He pulled his body into a crouch and peered at the covered windows. Even with the lights on, the blinds and the drapes should obscure their shadows.

Jane hoisted herself up to the couch and tucked one long leg beneath her. "The Bratva followed me home, knows where I live and wants that key—even though they probably don't even know I have a key. They just want me gone, off the case…if a laser beam is, in fact, what you saw."

"I know what a laser scope looks like. If there was no high-powered bullet behind it, then it was meant to scare you off, but I didn't feel like taking a chance and waiting to see what followed."

"Thanks, Tim. I thought…" She shook her head and pressed her fingertips against her temple.

"I know what you thought. C'mon, Jane. Give me a little credit here."

"I'm sorry. You have to admit. Your actions came out of nowhere. My first thought was not that you were saving me from a sniper."

He sat up, resting his back on the couch next to her leg, his head so close to her knee that he could lean against her. "We have to find out where he was. There are no houses out there?"

"There are houses, but they're not on my level. Like I said, he'd have to be in a tree, or—" she snapped her fingers "—the trail. A couple of hiking trails wind through the mountains. I suppose you'd be able to see my house from there. That would have to be some serious hardware, though, to shoot a bullet that far."

"The Bratva is fond of their Kalashnikovs. My friend Alexei has a few that could be accurate at that distance."

"You have strange friends." Jane stood up, waving her arms at the window. "I don't think anyone can see in now."

"I hope not, since you're making yourself a target." He wrapped his hand around her slim ankle and squeezed. "Maybe you shouldn't be tempting fate. Stay away from the windows."

"You're right." She slipped her foot from his grasp and crossed the room quickly to the kitchen. "I'll get your clothes out of the dryer, and you can change in the laundry room before you leave. No windows in there."

He snorted as he jumped to his feet. "You don't actually think I'm going to leave you here by yourself with a sniper out there, do you?"

She cocked her head at him. "I live here alone, so that's exactly what I'd expect."

"Jane, I'm not leaving. I'll spend the night outside on the balcony, if that's what it takes, but I'm not leaving tonight."

She crossed her arms over that ridiculously baggy tank top. "I'm a cop, Tim. I don't need your protection. I'm not one of your damsels in distress."

"I know. You're a big baddie with a gun, but the Bratva is no joke." He held up his hands. "If you kick me out, I'll curl up in one of those chairs on the deck like a stray cat and spend the night, anyway."

"I'm not kicking you out. Do what you need to do, but it's not necessary." She waved her hand toward the bedroom on this first floor. "Bed is made up in there. It's all yours, Sir Galahad."

"Thank you. I'm sure it's more comfortable than the Adirondack." But not half as comfortable as Jane's bed. "Extra toothbrush?"

"I have some from my dentist in the guest bathroom. Do you need anything else?"

He pointed to the laundry room. "If you don't mind, I'm going to wash my clothes and stick them in the dryer again. Now that I have the time, I'd rather not wear dry, dirty clothes."

"Knock yourself out. I'm going to bed, but I have to get to the station in the morning. If you're planning to take a hike tomorrow, you'll have to do it without me."

"I'll wait until you get off work. You're going to contact the harbor about Austin's key?"

"I will, but I'll have to log it into evidence first, and don't worry. I'll think up a good reason why I didn't report it at the crime scene." She turned at the bottom of the stairs. "What are you going to be doing?"

"I'll follow up on any of Austin's contacts in the area. Find out if the Bratva might be targeting anyone else in Austin's circle."

"Then we share."

He crossed his heart. "Share."

Tim watched her disappear up the stairs for several seconds, keeping his gaze pinned to the silent steps, just in case Jane returned with a last-minute invitation. Then he sighed and trudged to the laundry room.

What did a guy have to do to earn Jane's forgiveness?

THE FOLLOWING MORNING, Tim tried his hand at breakfast—scrambled eggs, toast and coffee from the fancy machine. He even managed to froth the milk.

As the toast popped up, Jane descended the staircase, fully dressed for work—no slouchy pajamas or bedhead to give him any images of a soft, sleepy Jane.

"You look great. I made breakfast."

She shook out the olive-colored jacket that had been over her arm and draped it over the back of the couch, grabbing the remote control on her way to the kitchen. "Thanks. You really didn't have to do this. I mean, you saved my life last night."

"And you saved mine at the docks, so I figured we canceled out each other's good deeds. But breakfast…"

he plucked the bread from the toaster and dropped it onto a plate of eggs, "...that's a whole other level."

Perching on the edge of a counter stool, she said, "I'm not making light of what you did last night, Tim. I'm sure you thought you saw a laser beam lighting up my forehead and took appropriate action."

"I didn't *think*. I saw it." He placed a plate of food under her nose. "You doubt me? Do you think I just pretended so that I could roll around on the floor with you?"

"You saw something." She pressed the buttons on the oversize remote, and the action at the French doors reversed course from last night, opening the room to the light of the canyon. "I just don't see how someone could've been out there."

"We'll find out later today. We still on for our nature hike?" He grabbed some salsa and orange juice from her fridge.

"I'm as curious as you are. I want to know if it's possible that someone was aiming into my house last night." She spooned some salsa onto her plate. "I'm just not so sure I'm ready to find out who it was."

"Bold move coming after a cop, for sure, but you don't know these people like I do. They'll do anything to protect their business. It's all about greed to them, just like any good gangster."

"Does the FBI know about Austin?"

"I told them last night after I left the park."

She toyed with her eggs. "Did anyone feel bad about not protecting him?"

"That's not what we were doing." He sipped his coffee through the foam. "We weren't following him to protect him. We were following him to find out what he knew about Bratva's activities in LA. If I had arrived earlier, I would've saved him."

"I know that." She tapped her coffee mug with her fingernail. "This isn't half bad. Maybe I should give that contraption to you."

"I don't have room for it in my kitchen." He sat on the stool beside her and forked a clump of eggs.

She dropped her lashes. "I don't know what your real kitchen looks like. I only visited you in Terry Rush's apartment in Mar Vista. Where do you even live?"

His hand shook a little as he picked up his cup. She couldn't let this go. "I live in Brentwood. I'll have you over some time."

She shrugged. "I gotta go. Thanks for breakfast. Can you let yourself out?"

"I can do that. Do you want to leave me a key, so that I can lock your dead bolt when I leave?"

"That's all right. The door is pretty sturdy." With half a piece of toast pinned between her teeth, she slid from the stool, placed her dishes in the sink and brushed crumbs from her fingertips.

She holstered her gun and took a bite of her toast. Waving the rest of it in the air, she said, "I'll keep you posted on Austin's container at the dock."

"Have a good one." She slammed the front door on the end of his sentence, and he dug his elbows into the counter on either side of his plate.

The best way to get back into Jane's good graces and

have a chance with her was to help her solve this case—even if that meant keeping a few more secrets from her.

LATER THAT DAY as Tim slumped at a desk at the FBI's office in the Federal Building in Westwood, Jane called him. He answered on the first ring. "Any luck?"

"Lots of luck. I finally reached the harbormaster's office in San Pedro. Austin Walker rented a storage container there last month. I sent the guy a picture of Austin's key, and he confirmed that it opened a storage container there—not that we even need the key now. The harbormaster could've opened it for us."

"Excellent." Tim pushed aside the waxy paper from his lunchtime sandwich and pulled a piece of paper to the center of his desk. "Where and when. I'll meet you there."

Jane paused for a couple of seconds. "I'll be at the harbor in a few hours, around three o'clock. I'll tell you which storage container is his when I see you there."

Tim twisted his lips. "Afraid I'll go out there and get the jump on you?"

"I'm not *afraid* of anything, but this is our lead, our damned case, and we'll run it."

He smothered a chuckle. "Yes, ma'am. I'll see you at the docks at three. You'll let me know if you get there any earlier?"

"I will."

She hung up before he could engage in any of his witty repartee. Maybe he should stop trying so hard. If he could get the woman off his mind for two seconds, that might be possible.

He crumpled the paper from his sandwich in one hand and shot it toward the wastebasket. At this time of day, it might take him a good hour to drive down to San Pedro. He'd finish his review of Austin's movements and then head down south. He wouldn't put it past Jane at this point to call him after she'd opened the container.

An hour later, he took off for San Pedro and beat Jane and the LAPD to the harbor. He doubted the harbormaster would give him the number of Austin's container even he did flash his FBI badge. He was certain Jane would've already warned the man about rogue FBI agents trying to nose their way into the investigation.

He parked his car in the lot and sauntered to the front gate. His phone buzzed with a text from Jane, letting him know they were on their way.

Fifteen minutes later, she pulled up with her partner in the passenger seat and a squad car behind them. On her way? She would've had him beat by forty-five minutes if he'd waited for her text.

When she stepped out of her unmarked sedan, she raised her eyebrows above her sunglasses but didn't seem surprised to see him, otherwise. He wished they didn't play these games with each other, but he wouldn't be the first one to quit.

She gave him a quick nod. "Damon, this is Special Agent Ruskin. Ruskin, this is my partner, Detective Damon Carter."

Tim thrust his hand out toward the stocky detective. "You can call me Tim."

Carter shot a quick glance at Jane before grasping

Tim's hand in a firm grip. "And I'm Damon. Good to meet you. I understand you're working the Russian Doll case from a different angle. Mob ties?"

"Russian Doll?" Tim shoved his sunglasses to the top of his head.

"For the tattoo." Damon patted his thigh.

"Yeah, mob ties, human trafficking." Tim gestured toward the office in the distance. "Do you need to check in with the harbormaster?"

Jane swung Austin's key around her finger. "He told us which container belonged to Austin and where it was located. We weren't too far off last night."

Pointing at the squad car, Tim asked, "Are the uniforms going to join us?"

"They're going to be our lookouts…just in case, and we have their car if we need to bag a lot of evidence from the container. I don't know what to expect, do you?"

"No clue." He patted Damon on the back. "I hope you're not squeamish, Damon."

Damon swallowed, his Adam's apple bulging in his throat. "A little."

"He's just playing with you, Damon. No reason to think there's anything…gruesome in that storage container." Jane charged ahead with both men in her wake.

As Jane slowed her pace, Tim drew up beside her and held out his hand. "Allow me to do the honors? I've been down this road before."

"I think I know how to open a storage container with a key." She closed her hand around the key, forming a fist.

Tim wiggled the fingers of his outstretched hand.

"I'm sure you're an expert at opening a container with a key, but the door might get stuck and you don't want to mess up your fancy suit."

Jane glanced at Damon, who was watching their exchange with widened eyes and twitching lips.

She blew out a breath and dropped the key into his palm. "Go for it, Ruskin. It's the second to the last one on the left."

Tim bobbled the key in his palm. Jane could think he just wanted to take control of the search, but his instincts made him leery of what…or whom they might find in the container.

He parked himself in front of the metal container, similar but smaller than the one where the Bratva had been keeping the caged women. Also, this one had a door that slid up instead of one that swung open—even more reason for him instead of Jane to open it. She really did look great in that olive suit with the crisp, pale yellow blouse.

Jane pocketed her sunglasses and studied the door as Damon hung back.

Tim shoved the key into the lock on the side of the container and clicked it open. Then he hunched forward and grabbed the door handle. He yanked it up.

As the metal squealed, Jane screamed. "Look out! Get back! Get back!"

Her warning was too late. As Tim scrambled to grab the handle and stop the door's upward progress, a wire dangled from the bottom of the door, teasing him.

He had no chance of stopping it, so he did the next best thing.

He launched himself backward, covering his face with his arm just before the explosion lifted him off his feet and threw him to the ground.

Chapter Eight

From a great distance, Jane heard Damon's voice calling her name. Did he need her help with something? A scream echoed in her ears, and she shook her foggy head. Had they been in a shoot-out?

"Jane, I'm going to move you. Can you hear me?" Strong hands gripped her beneath her arms, and someone dragged her body backward away from the intense heat.

She moved her lips and tasted ash. She tried to swallow and her throat caught fire. Fire. Explosion. Tim.

She struggled against the arms pulling her away from the leaping flames that filled the view from her squinting eyes. She croaked. "Tim."

"He's all right. Ambulance is on the way for both of you." Damon's face came into focus, the soot ringing his eyes black against his dark skin.

A hand circled her wrist. "I'm right beside you, Jane."

A sob choked her as she rolled her head to the side and met Tim's brown eyes, the bottom half of his face black and red, the ends of his hair singed.

"A-are you okay?"

"Outside of the ringing in my ears, my aching back, my sore head, my melting shoes and my scorched throat, I'm great. You?"

"Same."

Damon put a bottle of water to her lips. "Can you drink a little of this? One of the uniforms just brought it from his car."

Sirens wailed in the distance, and Jane pulled herself up to a sitting position, allowing a little bit of water to dribble into her mouth. It hurt too much to swallow. Fire engulfed Austin's storage container, plumes of black smoke streaming into the sky. The air tasted of soot and chemicals.

"We need to recover whatever we can." She tipped her legs to the side to hoist up to her knees, but Tim grabbed the waistband of her slacks.

"You're not going anywhere near that container until the fire department gets here and says you can." Tim scooted back and leaned against a container across from the one ablaze. He tugged on her pants. "Come back here with me, away from the heat. Damon's meeting the emergency vehicles at the entrance."

"They got to it, Tim. They got to it before we did." She pressed her shoulder against his. "I thought for a minute…"

"I know. I thought the same thing, but you saved me. You warned me. Idiot that I am, I didn't even think that the door could be rigged."

"It took me a few seconds to realize what that wire meant. A few more seconds…" She shivered despite the wall of flames across from her burning like a furnace.

"It didn't take you a few more seconds. You saw it, warned me and saved my life."

She patted his face. "Are you sure you're okay? I thought I saw you flying past me at warp speed."

He started a chuckle that turned into a cough. "That's what it felt like. I thought that blast was going to launch me into space. I covered my face and eyes to protect them."

"It worked." She traced a finger from his temple down to his chin, leaving a path through the soot. "That'll teach you to butt into my investigation and want to be first."

"I know. That was my punishment for being an ass." He fondled a lock of her hair, his fingertips crunching the singed ends. "Would you believe me if I told you I had a bad feeling about that container? I wanted to be there first—just in case."

"I would believe you because I had the same feeling. That's why I was eyeballing that door. Something felt off to me."

He offered his fist for a bump. "Here's to cop instincts."

"Are you two okay?" Damon returned, leading a stream of first responders, including a gleaming red firetruck cruising toward them.

"Nothing broken or burned beyond repair." Tim felt around his head. "A big lump on the back of my skull where I landed, though."

Two gurneys rolled up and snapped into place. A young EMT with anxious blue eyes and flushed cheeks asked, "Can you climb onto the stretcher, or do you need help?"

"Me?" Jane patted her chest. "I'm fine."

She scrambled to her feet and swayed to the side. "Maybe not."

The EMT steadied her and helped her onto the gurney. "Just lie back and relax. I'm going to check your vitals."

Jane glanced at Tim on a matching gurney, and he winked at her.

His wink made her blood pressure take a dive, just in time for the cuff the EMT was placing around her arm. "I'm okay, really. I need to take a look at the container once the fire's out."

Tim reached across and grabbed the bar of her gurney. "Anything that survived in the container is going to be too hot to handle for a while. Have one of the uniforms rope it off and stand guard. We can look through it once we get some of this gunk out of our lungs. I don't know about you, but my throat feels like hot sandpaper."

"Okay, but I'm not going to the hospital. I don't need to see a doctor." She glanced at the EMT as he released the blood pressure cuff from her arm.

"Your vitals seem fine, ma'am. You have a few burns that I'm going to treat with salve. Anything else you want to show me? Any injuries from the blast?"

"No." She didn't want to tell him about her confusion after the explosion. That was natural. She hadn't lost consciousness. She remembered every horrible second from the time she spotted the wire dangling from the slide-up door and Tim's inability to grab the door and stop it from opening. Once it opened, the explosion blew Tim off his feet and for a moment she thought she'd lost everything.

"A few abrasions, nothing more. I can treat those myself." She sat up, shrugging off the EMT's attentions. "I need to speak to the firefighter in charge. I'm sure the door was rigged to set off the explosion. I need to speak to the harbormaster, too. We need to check the cameras and see who planted that bomb and when."

"Whoa, there." Damon stood at the end of the gurney. "I'll handle the harbormaster. I already talked to Fire Captain Malone. He has our contact info. I'll get one of the uniforms to put up the tape."

"Sounds like your partner has things under control." Tim patted the bandage on the back of his head. "Let your patrol officers do their jobs. Damon can talk to the harbormaster and get the security footage while we search the contents of the container." He sat up and winced.

The older EMT hovering over Tim said, "Let me guess. You don't want to go to the hospital, either."

Tim swung his legs off the side of the gurney. "Naw, I'm all right. If I start seeing double, I'll check myself in. Feed me a couple of painkillers, and I'll be fine. I'll take care of the burns myself. Just give us some home remedies or over-the-counters for our throats, and we'll manage."

The EMT ripped the heart monitor from Tim's chest and muttered "Cops."

Damon patted Jane's shoulder. "You okay? You both gave me a scare."

"I'm fine, Damon. Thanks for your quick response. Go see about that security footage."

Once Damon left and Jane's EMT stopped fussing over her, she carefully stood up. "Thanks."

She took a few steps, and Tim slid his hand down her arm. He whispered in her ear. "Don't topple over, or he'll have us both flat on those stretchers again."

She leaned into him before they started walking toward the destroyed storage container. The flames had died out, and the smoke had dwindled to wisps.

Jane approached the firefighter giving orders and stuck out her hand. "I'm Detective Jane Falco with LAPD Homicide. This is FBI Special Agent Tim Ruskin. We were opening this container in connection to a case when it exploded. Did you find the source of the explosion?"

"Captain Joe Malone." He opened his gloved hand, revealing a black wire. "Like I told your partner, the door was rigged to a battery and some dynamite. You're lucky this piece of garbage didn't include any shrapnel in his bomb, or you two would've suffered a lot more than ringing eardrums, singed hair and sore throats. Of course, if one of you had ducked under the door while it was opening, I probably wouldn't be talking to you right now."

Jane put her hand to her neck. "Is your investigator going to check for prints on the bomb pieces?"

"We will, and we'll keep you informed. I have your partner's card." He jerked his thumb at the smoldering debris with white foam clinging to it. "If you're hoping to search through this mess, I'd give it at least another hour. You don't want to spark anything or get more burned than you already are. We can leave you a couple of pairs of heavy gloves for your search when you're ready."

"Appreciate that."

As the firefighters tamped down any remaining sparks in the container, one of the uniforms started ringing the area with yellow tape.

Jane glanced at his name tag. "Findley, can you stand guard until we're ready to search?"

"Yes, ma'am."

Tim cupped Jane's elbow. "We'll be back in an hour, Findley. Except for the firefighters, don't let anyone in there before us—including any other detectives. They need Detective Falco's permission first."

"Yes, sir. Got it." He took up a position in front of the yellow caution tape, his arms folded over his pumped-up chest.

Jane nudged Tim as they walked away. "I don't think anyone's getting past Findley."

"I agree." He steered her away from the docks. "An hour doesn't give us enough time to go back to your place or mine to clean up, so how about we go to a restaurant, drink lots of water and hit the bathroom there for a quick bath?"

"That's what I'll need to get this grime out of my skin." She plucked at her jacket. "Sadly, I think the suit you admired is done for."

"Nothing a good dry cleaning can't fix." He opened the passenger door of his car for her, and she slid onto the seat.

When he got behind the wheel, he flipped down the visor. "Wow, I look a lot worse than I feel."

She mimicked his actions on her side of the car, and her mouth dropped open when she caught sight of her soot-smeared face. "Those EMTs couldn't have given us something to clean our faces with?"

"Probably just paying us back for not wanting to ride in the ambulance with them." He punched the ignition button to start the car. "I'll let you have first dibs on the bathroom when we get to the restaurant. Can you find something nearby?"

She pulled her phone from her purse, which she'd left with Damon when she followed Tim to the container. As she searched for nearby restaurants, she said, "It's a good thing Damon stayed back so that someone had his wits about him after the explosion."

"Yeah." Tim bit his lip as he turned out of the parking lot. "Is he really squeamish? He might be in the wrong department, or the wrong line of work."

"He's new to Homicide, over from Vice. He hasn't been to an autopsy yet."

"Vice, huh? I never ran into him over there."

"I'm sure there's a lot of cops you haven't run into, especially as you were undercover." She tapped the window. "On the right, up ahead. Maybe they have some ice cream. I need something to soothe my throat."

"Ditto." He pulled into the parking lot of the chain restaurant. He reached into the back seat and dropped a box of tissues on the console. "We can make ourselves a little more presentable before we go inside. We don't want to scare anyone."

Jane plucked several tissues from the box and rubbed at the black ash on her face. "You didn't get a peek into the container before it exploded, did you? Boxes? Tools? Papers?"

"I didn't see a thing. But at least there were no people in there."

Jane shivered and wadded up the blackened tissues in her fist. "Did you expect there to be people in there?"

"I didn't know what to expect. There had been people in the one we raided and staked out before." He rubbed the back of his neck. "I had a prickling right here when I approached that container. I should've listened to it and proceeded with caution."

"I had the same feeling. That's why I was studying that door."

"At least one of us had some sense...and Damon." He squeezed her hand. "I'll order us some cool drinks and frozen desserts while you hit the ladies' room."

When they entered the half-empty restaurant, she left Tim at the table and made a beeline to the restrooms. Once inside, she shook off her jacket over the toilet, the ash and debris turning the water gray. She brushed off the rest of her clothing, her yellow blouse now a milky gray color.

At the vanity, she washed her hands and face, sucking in a breath every time the soap stung a burned area, and ran her fingers through her hair. She rinsed the fallout down the drain.

When she returned to the table, a glass of iced tea sparkled on her paper place mat, along with some water.

Tim cocked his head. "You don't look half bad."

"You still look like a raccoon. Are you sure your head's okay? Did the EMT check you for concussion?"

"It's fine." He exited from the booth. "I ordered us milkshakes, too. The waitress thinks we're insane."

When Tim left the table, Jane sucked down half the water at once. Then she drained her iced tea. By the time the waitress delivered their shakes, Tim emerged from the restroom, his face clean but dotted with red, scorched patches.

She shoved his shake in front of him. "You look like an adolescent suffering from an acute case of acne."

"Great." He shook his tea in front of him, rattling the ice, and took a sip. "Not a time in my life that I want to relive."

"Aww, did you get teased?"

He snorted and then grabbed his throat as if it hurt. "Other kids did not tease me. They were afraid of me."

"You were a badass?" Jane laced her fingers around her glass, suddenly realizing she probably didn't know the real Tim. Terry, his alter ego had indicated he hadn't enjoyed an idyllic childhood, and Tim seemed to confirm that later. After she'd found out he was an undercover FBI agent working her case—working her, she hadn't given him two seconds of her time to explain anything.

She watched his dark eyes change to shimmering pools as he stared over her shoulder, looking into his past.

"I was, but it wasn't just me they feared. They feared my father, my whole extended family."

Jane swallowed hard and then followed with a sip of the vanilla shake to soothe her throat. "Y-your extended family?"

"Jane, my father was the leader of the Brothers of Chaos in Riverside County. My extended family included the whole biker club." He spread his hands. "When I was Terry, I'd hinted at something in my past, but didn't want to go into details. Knowing Terry, you knew me, too. We weren't that different."

"Your alter ego rode a motorcycle. He wasn't in a biker gang." She toyed with her straw. Maybe it had been easier for him to interact with her under a different persona. Would she have bolted if he'd told her about his real background?

"How'd someone with your...past get beyond the FBI background investigators?"

"I had a mentor, someone who showed me the ropes and smoothed the way for me. James Kinney had been running a task force investigating my father's gang. Claimed he saw something in me." He blinked his dark lashes and shrugged. "Anyway, he steered me through the process."

She ran a fingertip through the condensation on the glass containing her milkshake. She wanted to ask more, but Tim had lost that dreamy look in his eyes. She didn't want to push her luck. What right did she have to question him now?

TIM LOOSENED THE grip he had on the edge of the table. Maybe if he'd told her all this stuff after she found out his true identity, they could've worked through the misunderstandings. He'd hated using his upbringing to garner pity or even fascination. It would've felt like another manipulation of Jane—and he'd never meant to play her.

Glancing at his phone, he said, "We're probably safe to sift through the container debris now. Finish up your shake, but not too fast. You don't want brain freeze."

She rapped her knuckles on the table, putting an exclamation point to the end of their discussion. "It did hit the spot. How's your throat?"

He pulled out his wallet. "Better. Yours?"

"Definitely better." She picked up her phone. "I haven't heard from Damon. I'm going to call him to see if he has anything on the security footage."

Jane listened for several seconds, and then left her partner a voice mail. "I'm thinking he didn't find anything, or he would've called."

Tim hadn't expected Damon to find anything useful. He didn't trust the guy. Tapping his finger on the stack of bills, he said, "That's it. Check is paid."

When they got in the car, Jane retrieved the gloves the fire captain had given them. "I guess if anything is too hot to handle, these should protect us."

Jane was too hot to handle, and he had no protection against her at all. She burned him every time he saw her. He jammed his knuckle against the engine button. "I hope there's something left for us *to* handle."

Fifteen minutes later, they approached the burnt-out container, the yellow tape stirring in the breeze from the water, Findley almost in the same position where they'd left him.

Tim pulled on the heavy-duty gloves, flexing his fingers. "Anything suspicious?"

"A few lookie-loos, but nothing more than that." Findley lifted the tape with one finger, and Tim and Jane ducked beneath it.

"Do you mind keeping watch a little longer while we go through the mess?" Jane eyed the scorched metal and the soggy debris on the ground. "Shouldn't take us too long."

"Happy to help out. My partner's been with Detective Carter. I think they went through the security footage."

Jane's head jerked up. "Anything?"

"Not that I know of, but I haven't seen them since they left."

"Thanks."

Tim crouched on his haunches and dug through the clump of ash, wadded paper and twisted metal outside the container.

Jane joined him, wrinkling her nose. "Anything salvageable?"

"Acrid smell, isn't it? Nothing here. I'm gonna check inside, not that there's an inside anymore." He rose to his feet and stepped across the threshold of what would've been the interior of the storage container. He nudged a few piles with the toe of his boot. "That explosion did a number in here."

Jane bent over and clamped her gloved hand around a scrap of metal. "I think this is part of the container itself, not the contents. Can you figure out what he had in here from this wasteland?"

"A lot of paper maybe, which is floating somewhere over the ocean now." Tim dragged his shirt up over his nose and mouth and trudged deeper into the pile.

Jane fanned out to the sides of the burned refuse, shuffling through the goopy debris. "Maybe some stuff got blown clear."

Using his gloved hands, Tim clawed through the wreckage, most of which disintegrated at his touch. Than his fingers met a few solid items in the ashy muck. He pinched the biggest object between his fingers and brushed aside the gunk to expose it.

His heart slammed against his rib cage as he pulled the gold chain free from its resting place, the ornate cross dangling in the air.

This had to be Lana's—did this mean she was dead?

Chapter Nine

Jane called over the space between them. "Did you find something?"

Tim shoved the cross into his pocket as Jane abandoned her corner and stepped over a scrap heap.

She crouched beside him and began to pick through the lumpy pile.

"Some solid objects. Things that survived the inferno." He cupped some misshapen jewelry in his palm.

"Something more than the metal from the container itself?" Jane bumped his shoulder and peered at his find. "What are those?"

He stirred the clumps of metal with his fingertip. "Looks like jewelry here. The fire had to have been hot to melt gold, but a few items survived."

Reaching over, Jane plucked a ring that had fused with a chain from his palm. "I'm bagging these. Do you want to give me whatever you shoved in your pocket? Or am I going to have to trick you out of that one, too?"

Tim closed his eyes and huffed out a breath. "I'm sorry. Bad habits die hard."

She narrowed her eyes and held out her hand. "Yeah,

that's why you have to kick some of those bad habits to the curb."

Tim dug the cross from his pocket and poured it into Jane's hand.

She gasped as she dangled the heavy chain from her fingertips, and the ornate cross swung in a hypnotic arc. "It's a cross. Looks like it sustained some damage. It has three horizontal bars, and the one at the bottom is bent or askew. Maybe it melted."

"It wasn't damaged. That's the way it's supposed to be. It's a Russian Orthodox cross. The final crossbeam on the vertical bar is always tilted."

She polished the jewels on the cross with her thumb. "How do you know that?"

"C'mon, Jane." He flicked his finger at the necklace. "I've been working the Russian mob scene for a while now. I learned Russian a while back, and I'm familiar with many of their icons."

"You speak Russian? What else don't I know about you?" She shook her head. "And why was your first instinct to hide the cross from me?"

"I... It might have something to do with the FBI's case." He braced his hands on his knees, eyeing the cross as if he didn't trust her not to drop it in her bag of goodies and spirit it away. Actually, he didn't.

"Why is it always the FBI's case when you want to keep something from me and *our* case when I have a lead for you?"

Tim spread his hands. "Sometimes things are just out of my control."

"I don't believe anything is ever out of your control, Tim."

As she pushed to her feet, Tim tugged on the sleeve of her soiled jacket. "We haven't discussed one of the most important elements of this explosion. How did Bratva, or whoever engineered this bomb, know which container was Austin's? They didn't know last night when they were staking out the place. They didn't know until the harbormaster contacted you with the information—and then beat you here."

Jane rubbed her nose, leaving a black spot on the tip. "I don't know. Did you tell anyone at the FBI?"

"No." He glanced at Findley standing guard. "I know you don't want to hear this Jane, but you may have someone in the department on the Bratva payroll. It's a common tactic of theirs, a way to stay one step ahead of law enforcement at all times."

"I hate even thinking about that." She shook her head. "You want me to keep quiet about the cross?"

"I know it's asking a lot. It's going against everything you learned at the academy, but you've also learned that there are bad cops. Hell, there are bad apples in the Bureau, too."

She leaned in toward him, her lips almost touching his ear. "I'll keep mum for now. Do you think this stuff was Natalya's? Why would Austin be keeping it here, and why would his killers be so desperate to get rid of it?"

"I'm not sure." He cupped his palm and tipped other pieces he'd found into the plastic bag Jane had flicked open. "This could be evidence of the women Bratva has or had in its clutches."

"Not worth much if it can't be identified. Is anyone even looking for these women? Natalya's family is back in Siberia. If the trafficked women are all Russian, their families may have no idea they're even missing."

He knew some families were looking...and desperate.

"Sad, isn't it?" Tim clapped his gloves together, sending up little eddies of ash, as if the air didn't have enough ash in it.

Jane shook the baggie of distorted jewelry where it clinked and rattled, as if trying to tell them a story. "And the Russian Orthodox cross? I assume you're keeping that."

"For now. There are a few things I want to check out."

"For now."

As they stepped away from the container, Tim took a deep breath of salty air. "Don't forget we have another assignment tonight."

"The hike?"

"The fresh air will do us good after this descent into hell." He ran his tongue along his teeth. "I'm going to be tasting smoke for the next week." He stuck out his hand toward Findley. "Thanks for keeping watch today."

"Just doing my job, sir. Do you need me for anything else, Detective Falco?"

"That's it, Findley. Thanks." Jane fished her phone from her jacket pocket. "I got a text from Damon. The footage is no use. There's nothing pointing at this particular row of containers. He's still working on identifying the cars in the lot, and viewing people moving around the docks."

"I wasn't holding out a whole lotta hope on that. This bunch got to Austin's storage container and rigged it with a bomb before you got here. They're not stupid enough to pose for the security cameras."

Shaking the baggie, Jane said, "I have to get back to the station. What time are you coming over for that other thing?"

Tim glanced at Findley, busy taking down the yellow tape. "Will you be ready by seven o'clock?"

"We're going out there at night?"

"The better to see what he saw in your window last night."

"The better to get eaten by mountain lions, too. I'll see you at seven." She turned to Findley and called out. "Hey, Findley, your partner and my partner left with my car. Can you give me a lift to the station?"

"Sure thing, Detective."

Tim whispered under his breath. "Tell him he can call you Jane. It's not gonna undermine your authority."

Jane cleared her throat. "You can call me Jane."

Findley whipped his head around, his cheeks red. "And you can call me Fin. Everyone at the department does."

"All right, Fin. Thanks again for your help."

"You got this cop comradery, kid." Tim squeezed her arm. "I'll see you tonight."

When Tim got to his car, he pulled the cross from

his pocket. The gold caught the setting sunlight and blazed to life. He hoped Lana was as alive as this cross.

He put it in his cup holder and tapped his phone. "Alexei, it's Tim."

WHEN JANE FINISHED DINNER, she popped another throat lozenge in her mouth. The taste could be better, but the menthol seemed to numb the soreness of her throat.

She'd logged the mutilated pieces of jewelry from Austin's container, minus the Russian Orthodox cross. She'd play along with Tim for the time being, but when was she going to learn she couldn't trust the man?

Couldn't trust him on this case. Couldn't trust him with her heart. Too bad he held her heart in his hands.

How had being a part of a biker gang affected him? She should've explored the opportunity to learn about the real Tim Ruskin at the time. Did growing up in that environment make him skittish about opening up?

She dragged her computer onto her lap and flipped it open. She entered Brothers of Chaos in the search engine, and then refined it to Riverside.

Several articles popped up, indicating the motorcycle gang was still active. She searched for Ruskin, Brothers of Chaos, and links to Tim's father populated the page. She clicked on one image and sucked in a breath.

Tim's father, Jack Ruskin, looked like a rougher, meaner, older version of Tim, but the resemblance was undeniable—until you got to the eyes. While Tim's eyes sparkled with humor and could form dark pools of compassion, Jack's flat eyes projected hostility and violence. She'd seen Aaron's eyes look exactly like that.

She shivered and then jumped when the doorbell rang. She closed the laptop on Jack Ruskin's malevolence, and strode toward the door. She peered through the peephole and opened the door for Tim.

He appraised her with a look, head to toe. "You clean up good."

"So do you." Her gaze skimmed over the black T-shirt that clung to his muscles and the dark jeans that outlined his flaring thighs. This guy never missed leg day.

Tim sniffed. "I can smell the menthol from here. I tried herbal tea and honey-lemon lozenges. Helped a lot."

"Yeah, I only feel like I swallowed one ashtray now." She tilted her head to the side. "Are you ready for a night hike?"

He hunched a shoulder, and a pack slid from his back. "Flashlight, binoculars, first aid kit, pepper spray, water. I think I have it covered. How'd it go at the station?"

"Nobody showed much interest in the jewelry, asked about a cross or stole the items from the evidence room, if that's what you were expecting." Jane crossed her arms. She didn't like that Tim had filled her head with suspicions about her coworkers. She'd had a hard enough time fitting in at the Northeast Division.

"That's not what I meant." He placed the backpack at his feet. "Did Damon find out anything about the cars in the parking lot? Any of the people on the docks this afternoon?"

"Not yet, but it doesn't mean he won't." She pointed to the flip-flops on her feet. "I'm going to put on some hiking boots. I'll be right back, and then maybe we can put your theory to rest."

Tim opened his mouth, but she'd turned her back on him and headed for the stairs. She didn't want to hear that it hadn't been his *theory*. He was positive he'd seen the red beam from a scope with his own eyes— she just wasn't sure she wanted to believe him, given the ramifications of that truth.

She kicked off her flip-flops and pulled on a pair of socks. She'd already taken her hiking boots from the closet and now she stepped into them, tightening the laces around her ankles.

She clunked down the stairs in her heavy boots, almost tripping on the last step as she saw Tim hunched over her laptop. She hadn't closed out the search on his father.

He glanced up at Jane, his face an unreadable mask.

Twisting her hands in front of her, she said, "I—I'm sorry. I looked up the Brothers of Chaos and your father after our conversation this afternoon."

He snapped the laptop closed. "And I'm sorry I accessed your computer. I was just going to search for something. Didn't realize you'd have anything up. Didn't intend to pry."

She took a tentative step into the room. "Why didn't you tell me any of that stuff?"

He shoved the computer from his lap. "Really? When did I have the opportunity to do that? In the few seconds I had before you blocked my number and all my access to your social media accounts? It doesn't matter. I wouldn't have used that to try to change your mind, and why would it? I didn't regret what I did, Jane. I did it for the job and the safety of my coworkers. I'd do it again. And I don't regret falling for you, either. That was real."

"Let's get going before it's too late." She lifted a dark hoodie from the back of a chair and shoved her arms in the sleeves. "I know where we can park to access the trailhead. It's not too far from here."

Tim pushed up from the couch and swept up his pack from the floor. "You're bringing your weapon, I hope."

"Locked and loaded." She patted her own backpack. She insisted they take her car, as she knew the way.

Before they walked out of the house, Tim turned and studied the room. "This is just the way it was last night— blinds open, those two lamps on. We want to see what he saw."

Jane hunched her shoulders against the chill snaking up her spine and locked the door behind them.

Five minutes later, Jane maneuvered the winding roads in Benedict Canyon, her high beams illuminating the dark turns. Most of the houses here hid behind tall hedges, tall gates or both, invisible to the casual driver. Aaron had picked out the house on his own as a surprise for her. For once he'd gotten it right. The location had suited her much more than it had him. That was one reason why he'd let it go easily in the divorce. The other was to keep her quiet about his violent outburst, keep her from pressing charges against him.

Sighing, she made the last hairpin turn and pulled her car off the road and into an outlet. During the weekends, hikers' vehicles crowded the sides of the road here, but nobody was foolish enough to hike this trail at night.

"It's dark out here." Tim cracked open his door. "Someone went to a lot of trouble to scope out your house."

"We're here to see if that's even possible." Jane reached into the back seat and grabbed her pack. She stood at the trailhead, adjusting the straps.

Tim slung his own pack over his shoulder and shoved his gun in the pocket of his black jacket. "How far do you think we have to hike in before we can see the back of your house?"

"Shouldn't be more than a mile. Just keep your flashlight trained on the ground ahead of you. I don't want to send for emergency vehicles or have to hike into a canyon to rescue you."

He chuckled. "You rescued me once today. Is that your limit?"

"I should've done more, should've warned you sooner about that wire."

"You saved me from ducking under that door. That's good enough for me." He squeezed her shoulder. "You lead the way."

Jane stomped her boots against the dirt and aimed her flashlight at the trail two feet in front of her. "Follow me."

The trail narrowed to single file quickly and Tim dropped behind her, his heavy breathing stirring the hair at the back of her neck, his sneakers crunching the earth as he dogged her steps.

As her legs pumped up the incline, her own breathing began to rasp through her nose and mouth, stinging her throat again. She grabbed the branch of a tree. "Can we stop for a minute? Turns out breathing heavily is murder on your throat after inhaling smoke and ash."

"Yeah, who would've imagined that?" Tim twisted around and lifted his water bottle from the side of his pack.

They both stood for several seconds, glugging down water as the bushes rustled beside them with night creatures scuttling away from this unwelcome intrusion.

Tim dug in his pack and withdrew his binoculars. He hung them around his neck and lifted them to his face. "I can already see a few houses through the trees, but not yours. You wanna have a look?"

Because the binoculars were around his neck, Jane had to lean in toward him to peer through the lenses. She could still detect a hint of smoke beneath the fresh scent of his bodywash. Her lashes fluttered for a second, and she couldn't focus on anything through the binoculars.

She pulled away from him. "Not yet. We should be able to see my house around the next curve, which is straight up, unfortunately."

"I'm right behind you." He let the binoculars drop to his chest with a thump as he adjusted his backpack.

Jane coiled her thigh muscles and dug in for the ascent. The mountain lions might think they were too loco to bother.

After several minutes, they rounded the bend and a clump of trees. When they got clear of the trees, a flat ridge jutted out from the trail.

"Here." Jane shuffled onto the ridge, watching the ground. "We should be able to see my house from here."

"Makes total sense." Breathing a little easier than Jane was, Tim drew up beside her, his shoulder pressing against hers. "This would be a place where you could focus and maybe train a sniper rifle."

Jane crossed her arms over a stomach tied into knots. She'd been entertaining Tim before, but he could've been right.

He raised his binoculars and swore. "This is it, Jane. I can see the glass doors of your deck with just these binoculars. A high-powered rifle would have no trouble extending into your house."

He dropped to the ground and rolled onto his stomach.

"What are you doing?" She nudged him with the toe of her boot.

"Mimicking the position of a sniper." He scooted forward on his belly, and Jane's heart skipped a beat.

"Do not venture any farther. You're going to drop off the edge."

"I've seen all I needed to see to confirm my initial belief last night." He scrambled back from the drop-off, but remained on the ground. "Someone had you in his sights from this location. If I hadn't noticed the red laser, he could've taken you out."

"You proved your point." Jane hugged herself. "Can we leave now?"

Tim's flashlight lit up the ground as he ran his hand over the dirt. "Maybe he left something behind."

"You're going to tell me Bratva is the only group that would have the motivation and resources to stalk me this way, aren't you?"

"Probably, but you might be safe for now."

"Really?" Jane's gaze darted around the dark trail, her blood running cold more from the human predators than the animal kind. "I don't feel safe—at all."

Stabbing a white object with a twig, Tim scrambled to his feet. "Last night they wanted to stop you from making any discoveries related to Austin's key. They managed to do that today. Bratva could be lying low, watching your next move."

"That's just great." She flicked the cigarette butt skewered on the stick. "Do you think that belongs to my sniper?"

"I do." He slipped it into his pocket.

"Even if you test that for DNA, I'm not sure how it's going to help us unless we get a suspect—and those are in short supply right now."

"Maybe for you, but we've collected DNA one way or another from most of the Bratva gang members in LA."

"Matching that cigarette to one of the rogues in your gallery isn't going to prove anything. These are public trails. Anyone can hike them. The most you could get him on is smoking in the canyon, which isn't allowed. Unfortunately, even grand theft isn't prosecuted here in LA anymore. Can you imagine how *this* crime would go over?"

"It's not about bringing charges, Jane." He stuffed his binoculars into his backpack and jumped from the ledge to the trail. "It's about applying pressure. It's a game, almost."

"I don't want to play that game. This means I need to keep my blinds closed at night."

"Not a bad idea for a while." He finished the rest of his water. "At least the hike back is downhill."

On the way back to the car, they exchanged very few words as they concentrated on safely maneuvering the trail. Descending could be more precarious than ascending when you had to fight against gravity.

When they reached the car, they slung their packs into the back seat. Tim patted his pockets at the passenger door and grunted.

"I lost that cigarette butt. It must've fallen right out of my pocket." He pivoted and pointed his flashlight at the trailhead. "It's not far. I checked for it when we were almost at the end."

"Is it that important?"

"It is to me. I want to see if I can match the DNA to someone we have on file." As he headed back toward the trail, he said over his shoulder, "Wait in the car. I'll be right back."

Jane had transferred her gun from her backpack to the pocket of her hoodie on the hike. She pulled it out now and crept to the trailhead. She'd wait out here for Tim—just in case. A single hiker was a bigger target for predators—both animal and human.

Something crashed through some branches, and Jane snapped to attention. She flicked her flashlight at the trailhead. Then twigs crackled behind her, and she started to turn—but she didn't get far.

Someone cinched her midsection, trapping her arms against her body. A hand clapped over her mouth.

A rough voice grated against her ear. "If you hurt him, I'll kill you."

Chapter Ten

Jane couldn't tell if her attacker had a weapon or not—
his body was lethal enough. Her own gun was pinned
helplessly to her hip where the man had his arm clamped
against her body.

She bucked and thrust her elbow back, making contact with hard flesh.

He released a soft gasp but tightened his grip. He
growled in her ear. "Tell me what you did to him? Where
is he?"

Jane's brain tried to sort through his words, but they
made no sense. Who was he looking for and what did
he think she did with him? The hand across her mouth
made any questions impossible. Why was he asking her
questions?

She had to warn Tim. She kicked her legs up in the
air, slamming the heel of her boot against his shin.

He let loose with a stream of expletives in a foreign
language, and his hand slipped from her mouth.

Jane screamed. "Tim, watch out!"

"What the hell is going on here?" Tim burst from the

trailhead, his gun in front of him, his flashlight balanced on his wrist, illuminating the scene.

Her assailant released her, his hands shooting skyward. "Tim, it's me. It's Alexei."

Tim responded in Russian and then followed it with English. "What the hell are you doing with Jane?"

Jane stumbled against the car, her gun dangling at her side. "You know this creep?"

"You know this wild woman?" Alexei pointed at Jane, his eyes wide below the black beanie on his head.

"Let's start over." Tim holstered his weapon in his waistband. "Jane Falco, this is Alexei Savchenko, a buddy of mine. Alexei, this is Jane, an LAPD homicide detective and my…friend."

Alexei hit his forehead with the heel of his hand. "I'm so sorry, Jane. I followed Tim here. When I saw you out here with your gun and no Tim, I thought you did something to him."

"You're lucky she didn't do something to you." Tim brushed past Jane and gave Alexei a bear hug. "Good to see you, man. And what do you mean you were following me?"

"Sorry." Alexei peeled the cap from his head and ran his fingers through his long, dark hair. "I had an app tracking your phone from…" he glanced at Jane "…our last assignment. I never took it off. I didn't use it, though—not until I got your message."

Alexei stepped around Tim and hugged Jane. "Sorry. Friend of Tim is friend of mine."

She wriggled out of his grasp and sniffed. "I'm not sure I can say the same."

He cocked an eyebrow at her. "Came in too rough, huh?"

"You came in. Period. Why didn't you just approach me like a normal person and ask me about Tim?"

Alexei's nostrils flared, making him look almost feral. "I'm not normal person."

Even with his identity sorted out and Tim standing a few feet from her, Jane felt a flicker of something primal in her gut—a reaction to this man. She could believe he wasn't a normal person.

Then Alexei's face cracked into a smile and he spread his hands. "I know Tim from some dangerous operations. I thought his life was in danger, and I saw you standing here with gun in your hand. You not a normal person, either."

"Now that we've established that none of us is normal, let's get away from this trail before more abnormal people show up—the real dangerous ones." Tim held up the cigarette butt. "At least I found this."

"Evidence?" Alexei squinted his eyes.

"Could be." Tim put his find into the front pocket of his backpack. "How'd you get here, Alexei? I don't see a car."

"I parked down the road."

Tim turned to her and asked, "Jane, can he follow us back to your place? We can explain further."

"I'm gonna be all ears, since you seem to have been keeping Alexei out of the picture, and it sounds like he may be very much a part of this case."

"Tim's private like that. He likes to—how do you say it in English? Compartments?"

"Close enough." Jane opened the car door and placed her weapon on the console. "Alexei, you can follow me back to my house, or I guess you can just follow Tim's phone."

"I'll follow you, Jane."

Before she slid behind the wheel, she wagged her finger between the two men. "And don't start speaking Russian between you to cut me out."

Alexei saluted and slipped away into the night as quietly as he'd come upon her.

Ten minutes later, Jane pulled into her driveway, steering around Tim's car. She didn't see Alexei's car, and his headlights had dropped off before they got to her house, but he walked up behind them.

Running into Tim's friend was a more important development than verifying Tim's assertion that a sniper had been taking aim at her last night through her window. So they'd confirmed that. Now what? Now she had to be afraid in her own home. Now she had to shut out the very view that gave her peace.

When she put the car in Park, Tim reached over and grabbed her hand. "Are you all right? Alexei is special ops, if you haven't figured that out. He wouldn't have hurt you without determining the situation first."

She looked into his eyes. "What Alexei did doesn't bother me as much as what you did, or didn't do. How can I trust you when you're always keeping secrets from me?"

He sighed. "Sometimes, Jane, they're not my secrets to tell."

Alexei rapped on the window, and they both jumped.

Jane exited the car and leaned in to retrieve her pack.

Alexei inhaled beside her. "This is beautiful spot. It smells like Polisia back home."

"You're Ukrainian, not Russian?"

"That's right." He raised his hands, palms out. "Not KGB, I promise."

"I thought there was no KGB, anymore."

Alexei lifted his eyebrows. "It's FSB now. Different name, same organization. Same thing for Bratva. Just another name for Vor y Zakone. As if renaming these organizations can change what they do. Same dark deeds."

His eyes glittered, again resembling some wild predator.

Tim came up behind her and squeezed her shoulder. "Let's talk about those dark deeds inside."

The two men spoke in Russian behind her as she led the way to her front door. When she walked inside, she immediately crossed the room to pull her blinds and drapes.

Tim jerked his thumb in her direction. "Last night someone aimed a laser at Jane through those glass doors. They did it from the spot where we just hiked."

"That's far." Alexei peeked through the blinds. "Sniper rifle. I know Kalashnikov that could make that distance."

"Do you also know a shooter who could take the shot?" Tim hung his pack over the back of a chair in Jane's dining room.

"A few." Alexei formed his fingers into a gun and pulled an imaginary trigger. "Including me."

Jane licked her lips, not completely trusting Tim's friend. Why did she have a spy in her house and snipers out her window? Would she ever have been a target if Tim hadn't inserted himself into her investigation? "Do either of you want anything to drink?"

"Water fine for me." Alexei thumped his chest with his open palm.

"Nothing for me, Jane." Tim grabbed the same chair where he'd draped his pack and spun it around, straddling it.

Holding out her still trembling hand, she said, "I guess I'm the only one still rattled by what happened."

"Sit down." Tim hopped out of his chair. "I'll get Alexei's water and a glass of wine for you."

With her knees stiff, Jane lowered herself into a chair at the table while Alexei took the one across from her.

"I'm sorry, Jane. I thought you were waiting for my friend. I saw your gun—" he shrugged "—and reacted the way I always do with gun."

"Remind me to keep mine holstered at all times around you." She folded her arms on the table, rubbing her upper arms with both hands.

Alexei threw his head back and laughed. "I like your friend, Tim. She cool lady."

"She is cool lady." Tim placed a wineglass in front of her with a generous pour of red practically lapping at the rim and slid Alexei's water to him.

Jane folded her hands around her glass, shifting her gaze from Tim to Alexei. "Which one of you is going to tell me why Ukrainian special ops is interested in the murder of a Russian woman, possibly connected to a human trafficking ring?"

"Ukraine always interested in Russian mob around world, especially US." Alexei spread his large hands on the table. "We work with FBI, sometimes CIA. Our best interest to stop their criminal activity…especially when it involve Ukrainian women."

"But Natalya wasn't Ukrainian. She was Russian." Jane ran a thumb down her glass to the stem.

Tim cleared his throat. "Natalya wasn't trafficked. She was murdered."

"The other women Bratva is trafficking are Ukrainian and Natalya just found out about it?" Jane took a big gulp of wine to dispel the sour taste on her tongue. "That's why you think they took her out? Austin, too?"

Alexei's dark eyes widened. "Austin?"

"Oleg Stepanchikov." Tim wiped a hand across his mouth, as if to wipe away the name he'd uttered.

Alexei dropped his head and slammed his fist on the table.

Jane's gaze darted to Tim's face. "What's wrong? Does Alexei know Oleg… Austin?"

"He…" Tim trailed off and took a swig of her wine.

Alexei's head shot up, and he clenched his hands. "I contacted Oleg about looking into sex trafficking ring. I got him killed. I got his girl killed."

"You can't blame yourself, Alexei. The Bratva would've involved him one way or the other. We both know it. At least you had him on the right side. They've been trying to involve him for years to offer him protection against his father's enemies. The kid was doomed."

Alexei rubbed his eyes. "Maybe you right."

Jane sat forward in her seat. "If Alexei is involved in all this, you should show him the cross—the one you found in the container."

"Cross?" Alexei's head jerked up. "What's this cross?"

Tim bit his lip, his gaze shifting from Jane to Alexei. "Austin led us to a storage container at the docks."

"Container, like other container?" Alexei's eyes widened, and his mouth tightened into a grimace.

Jane shot a glance at Tim. Alexei seemed to know as much about the case as she did. Tim must've been filling him in, so why his reluctance now to show him the necklace?

"Not quite like the other. Same location, but this container was small. The other was more like a warehouse."

"No cages?" Alexei wiped a shaky hand across his forehead. "No chains."

"Nothing like that."

Jane wrinkled her nose. "Not that we know of, anyway. Someone blew up the place before we could get a good look."

"Blew it up?" Alexei's hands mimicked an explosion. "Before you go there?"

"The door was rigged to set off an explosive device. We opened it and—" Tim copied Alexei's hand motions "—boom."

"Explain a lot." Alexei pointed to Tim's hands, sporting red welts from his burns.

Tim studied his hands as if he'd never seen them before. "I'm pretty sure the container was too small for cages—or people."

"Probably." Jane rolled the wineglass between her palms. "But the fire that followed the blast didn't destroy everything."

"The cross? You find cross." Alexei pressed his palms together as if in prayer.

Tim answered, "We did, along with some other twisted pieces of metal, maybe other pieces of jewelry."

"But the cross. Show him the cross, Tim" Jane snapped her fingers. "This piece was intact."

Tim blew out a long breath and pulled the necklace from his pocket. He dangled it from his fingers in front of Alexei, the gold cross catching the light, providing a glittering background for the dusky jewels.

Alexei reached for it, his hand shaking. "It's hers. It's Lana's."

Jane blinked. "Who's Lana?"

Tim poured the necklace into Alexei's outstretched palm. "Lana is Alexei's sister. I've been looking for her for the past few months."

Chapter Eleven

Jane took a gulp of her wine—not that the ruby liquid warming her throat would help her swimming head. As usual, Tim had been playing the game on some other level—one that he hadn't bothered to share with her. Was he even working this case on behalf of the FBI, or had he gone rogue?

She cleared her throat and reached out to squeeze Alexei's fist clenched around his sister's necklace. "I'm so sorry, Alexei. Does the Bratva have her?"

Alexei dropped his chin to his chest. "Lana came to US a few months ago. Overstayed visa and work at Russian club as waitress, get paid cash under table. Is that what you say?"

"Yeah, under the table so she doesn't pay taxes." Jane folded her hands. "What happened at the club?"

"She disappear." Alexei snapped his fingers. "Like that."

Glancing at Tim, Jane asked, "Where is this club?"

"Hollywood. North Hollywood. Where else? Many Russian immigrants there—and Ukrainians like Lana."

"When did she go missing?" Jane had switched

smoothly into cop mode, putting her irritation with Tim on hold—for the moment. "Was she last seen at the club? How long had she been working there?"

Pinching the bridge of his nose, Alexei squeezed his eyes closed. "She came here about three months ago. She got job at Ivan's first week or two, through friend. Maybe one month ago, I couldn't reach her. I warn her about that place. No good."

"We're pretty sure Bratva owns Ivan's, or at least gets protection money from them." Tim crossed his arms over his chest as she narrowed her eyes at him. "We know they run business from the club—drugs, for sure. There was an incident several months ago where an MS-13 gang shot up the place in a dispute over territory."

"Have you tried to infiltrate it?" Jane ran a thumb around the rim of her glass.

"The FBI hasn't. Maybe you could tell me if LAPD has. We don't have any proof to go in and shut things down."

"And the women?" Jane swallowed a lump in her throat. "Do you think they're running women out of that club?"

Tim hunched his shoulders up to his ears. "Probably, but we can't get inside. We tried to install a female agent there once, but the management didn't bite. They wouldn't hire her."

"What about Lana's friend? Does she still work there?"

"Maria?" Alexei rubbed his eye. "She long gone. I tried to call her when I came out to look for Lana, but her phone go to voice mail. I don't know where she live."

"Have you been to Ivan's?" Jane's gaze darted between Tim and Alexei as they exchanged a look. "What?"

"I'm not welcome at Ivan's, anymore." Alexei spread his big hands wide. "And they know Tim federal agent. We can't get close."

"I guess that leaves the LAPD." Jane drummed her fingers against the bowl of her glass. "Maybe we've already checked out the place. I can start by asking the management about Lana. They can't ban me."

"Don't say my name, or they'll try." Alexei clasped the back of his neck. "I got a little aggressive when I was there."

"I'll remember not to get aggressive." She shot a look at Tim. "I suppose you can't come with me. Were you aggressive, too?"

"Not really, but once they knew I was there they clammed up. Nobody would talk to me."

Jane nipped her bottom lip. "The LAPD could make it hard for them to do business until they cough up some information. Those clubs are always in violation of one thing or another. We could nitpick."

"I would appreciate, Jane." Alexei juggled the necklace in the palm of his hand. "I keep this?"

"I was going to give it to you, anyway. That's why I called." Tim squeezed Alexei's shoulder. "I figured it's proof that Lana is mixed up with Bratva. Austin kept that container at the dock for some reason. Maybe he was gathering proof against Bratva."

Jane said, "He should've made his move sooner. Those two—Natalya and Austin—knew something. I just wish they would've come to us…or the FBI."

"Or me." Alexei pounded his chest with his fist. "Austin was getting that proof for me."

"Looks like he got it." Jane leveled her finger at the cross glittering in Alexei's hand.

"But what does it mean? Where is Lana? She must've been in warehouse you raided, Tim." Alexei had jumped up, pouring the necklace from one hand to the other.

Tim joined him and clapped his hand on Alexei's broad shoulder. "We have no proof. That necklace is the closest I've been to Lana, yet. The only thing that ties her to Bratva's trafficking besides working at Ivan's."

"I'll get Ivan to tell truth one way or another way." Alexei slammed his fist, still clutched around the necklace, into his palm.

"Whoa." Jane waved her hands in the air. "You're not going back to Ivan's, and is there really an Ivan?"

Tim answered. "Ivan Kozlov owns and operates Ivan's. We think he has Bratva backing but no proof."

"You two—" Jane wagged her finger between Tim and Alexei "—stay away from that place. I'll take my partner with me tomorrow and question Ivan and anyone else I can corner. I can probably get more information than you two." She turned to Tim. "Is there any connection between Natalya and Ivan's? Any excuse I can give for asking questions there?"

Tim shrugged. "You can pretend there is. Tell them you found a matchbook from Ivan's in Natalya's house. Now you're investigating two people from that house that have been murdered."

"I'll pay them a visit tomorrow." Jane stifled a yawn.

"I let you go." Alexei stuffed his sister's necklace in his pocket. "I keep this."

Jane moved toward her front door. "Where did you park? I didn't see your car."

"Down the road, in cubby. Out of the way." He tapped her shoulder. "I'm sorry. I didn't mean to scare you. Just looking out for my brother, Tim."

"Apology accepted. Do you need a ride to your car?"

"I'll walk. You two sort out…business." Alexei winked at Tim before walking out of the house.

Had Alexei, even in his overwrought state, sensed the tension between her and Tim?

Jane shut the door behind him, and leaned her forehead against it for a second before spinning around. "Does the FBI even know you're investigating the disappearance of Lana?"

Tim widened his stance, looking ready for battle. "I'm working a human trafficking case we're building against Bratva. The FBI, not just me, raided a warehouse on the docks in San Pedro on a tip, and we found evidence that people had been held there against their will. All of that is true."

"Does the Bureau know about your personal connection to one of the possible victims?"

"No. That's not necessary for them to know."

"What about me?" Jane tapped her chest. "You didn't think that was necessary for me to know? We're supposed to be in this together, but you still withhold information from me. I just don't understand why. Your excuse before was that you didn't trust anyone, including the LAPD, because you think someone is passing info along to Bratva. Fair enough, but I don't see where Lana's disappearance falls into this category of secrecy, unless…"

"Unless what?"

"Unless Alexei's sister means more to you than some missing victim, and this is some personal project for you." Jane clasped her hands in front of her and tried not to worry her fingers. She wasn't usually the jealous type. God knows, Aaron had had his affairs when they'd been married, and after a while she hadn't given one damn. But the thought of Tim rushing headlong in to protect another woman the same way he'd tried to protect her made her heart stutter.

He shoved his hands in his pockets and hunched his shoulders. "It is a personal project for me…because Alexei is like a brother to me, and that makes Lana family. I met her only once or twice at Alexei's family's home in Kyiv. Darling girl who wanted to see the world."

"I'm sorry. I'm sorry for Alexei and the rest of Lana's family. But why not tell me, Tim?"

He scratched his chin and sank to the arm of her couch. "It's habit, Jane. Sort of self-preservation. I always feel like I have to keep something to myself, just in case."

"In case of what?" Her insides softened for the boy who grew up with a motorcycle gang as a family that taught him to distrust everyone. And in the end, it was his own family he couldn't trust.

"Just in case someone can take it and use it against me." He clasped the back of his neck and raised his eyes to the ceiling.

"I—I would never..." Jane stopped when Tim pinned her with a dark gaze. "I broke it off with you because you lied to me, Tim. You used me."

He opened his mouth and then snapped it shut. "Be careful at Ivan's tomorrow. I don't trust anyone over there. You're already on Bratva's radar, and I guarantee Ivan and his cohorts at the club know that, or they will as soon as they report your visit to whomever is controlling operations there."

She accepted his change of subject, and the knots loosened in her belly. "I will be careful. Is it a nightclub? Bar? Will it be open during the day?"

"It's a combination restaurant/bar. The restaurant opens for dinner at five. The nightclub is upstairs and kicks off when dinner is winding down, around nine o'clock."

"The nightclub is not like strippers, is it?" She wrinkled her nose. She was all for women supporting themselves as they deemed necessary, but the vibe in those clubs depressed her.

"No, nothing like that. The cocktail waitresses upstairs are fully clothed, and there's usually some music. I'm pretty sure Lana worked as a cocktail waitress and not a dinner waitress. What time are you going over there?"

"I'll show up when they open for dinner. Maybe I can talk to some of the workers."

"Good luck with that." Tim pushed up to his feet. "Thanks for coming out with me tonight. I'm sorry Alexei gave you a scare."

"We got so sidetracked with Alexei's drama that we

didn't look at your evidence. You said you found the cigarette butt."

Tim fished in his pocket and withdrew the plastic bag. "I got it. We have DNA from a lot of Russian mobsters and their lackeys here in LA. Maybe I can find a match."

Leaning forward, Jane squinted at the bag. "Lemme see that."

He released the bag and she dangled it in front of her face. She breathed out. "Is that lipstick?"

He huddled close, his head next to hers. "Looks like it."

"Well, that's probably useless, unless you know any female snipers."

Tim snatched the bag from her fingers. "As a matter of fact...I do."

Chapter Twelve

Tim's blood rushed to his head and he sat down heavily on the arm of the couch again. He didn't know whether his light-headedness came from the realization that the sniper could be Azra Balik, or that he'd readily admitted to Jane that he did, indeed, know of a female sniper.

Her mouth formed an O. "You're kidding me. Now I feel bad for being sexist and assuming there were no women in the sniping business. Who is she?"

He pinched his chin. "Her name is Azra Balik. She's Turkish. The Russians have used her before."

"That's great." Jane's gaze flicked to the closed drapes. "They hired a professional sniper to take me out? What are my chances of getting through this investigation alive?"

"We can't be sure it's her." He jiggled the bag. "This may not even belong to the sniper."

"We're still talking about a sniper here, aiming a scope through my window. Whether the shooter is a he or a she, Turkish, Russian or Icelandic is not really the point, is it?" She rubbed her arms. "I've had criminals unhappy with me in the past, but this is a whole other level."

"They're trying to intimidate you, Jane. They understand that murdering a police officer is, like you said, a whole other level. They don't want it to get to that."

"That makes two of us." She rubbed her eyes, smearing a bit of mascara down her cheek.

"You look tired. It's been a long night at the end of an even longer day." He put the bag with the cigarette back in his pocket. "We both have our assignments for tomorrow. I'm going to look into this cigarette butt and the current whereabouts of Azra Balik. You need to process the items and information about the explosion at Austin's container. Your team can get a handle from the fire department on the type of explosive used and all that, right?"

"I'm sure they're on it, already. I'm taking those pieces of jewelry we found in the debris to Ivan's with me."

Tim whistled. "You're going in hot. They'll probably toss you out as fast as they tossed me out. Be careful."

"Careful is my middle name." She put her hand over her heart.

Tim folded his arms, bunching his fists under his armpits. Careful enough to let him stay the night again?

He lifted his shoulders. "I could camp out in the guest bedroom again tonight."

She spun away from him and grabbed her empty wineglass from the table. "I don't think that's necessary. We know there's nobody out on the trail tonight."

He blew out his disappointment on a harsh breath.

"Okay, Jane *Careful* Falco. Lock up and keep your gun handy."

She looked up from rinsing her glass at the sink. "I always do."

His eyebrows jumped. "Even when your life isn't being threatened by Russian mobsters?"

"Always." This time she kept her head down, concentrating on the glass.

Did she still fear her ex? He stared at her stiff shoulders for a second. "Good to know. We'll touch base tomorrow...and I'm glad you know all about Lana now. I know you don't need a reason to make your work personal, but when you know the victims..."

She snapped a towel from the oven handle and wiped her hands. "I know. Just don't let your connection to Lana's brother make you throw caution to the wind."

"Caution is *your* middle name—not mine."

She retorted. "I'm careful. You can be cautious."

He winked and raised his hand as he let himself out.

He got into his car and backed out of her driveway. As he made his way down the hill, another car on the side of the road flashed its lights.

Tim's nostrils flared as he slowed down and slid his weapon from the console into his lap. When he pulled abreast of the car, he huffed out a breath.

Alexei made the universal sign of rolling down a window, and Tim powered down the passenger-side window and leaned across the seat. "You still here?"

Alexei held up his phone. "Checking messages. Surprised to see you. Wasn't sure you'd be leaving that house, that woman. Although it's obvious you didn't tell her about Lana."

"You know I like to keep things close to the vest." At Alexei's puzzled expression, Tim clarified. "I don't like to tell anyone everything I know."

The Ukrainian dropped his chin to his chest. "I know, but good woman hard to find. Jane is a good woman... and kickass."

Tim laughed. "That she is. Where are you staying? You need a place?"

"Hotel in Hollywood. I have other business here." Alexei held his finger to his lips.

"Business, huh?" Tim made a gun out of his fingers and pointed it at Alexei. "You don't tell everyone everything, either, brother."

"You not beautiful, kickass woman."

Tim buzzed up his window and left Alexei's car in a cloud of dust.

He hoped he wouldn't live to regret telling Jane about Lana—of course, he hadn't told her everything about Alexei's sister. Hadn't told Alexei everything, either.

JANE SLUMPED AT her desk at the Northeast Division and listened to Damon's voice mail for the second time. Looked like she'd have to hit Ivan's by herself.

Damon had been gung ho to accompany her to the club, but had backed out at the last minute to take care of an issue with his kids. She rubbed her chin. Was her partner using his kids to get out of work assignments? He did thorough work—when he did it.

She'd have to have a heart-to-heart with him about

how to get ahead in Robbery-Homicide. Strange, as she'd heard nothing but good reports of his time in Vice. If he wanted a career like that slug, Marino, he could continue along the same path he was on now. If he wanted to rocket to the top like Jake McAllister and Billy Crouch, he'd better get on board.

She gathered her purse, jacket and briefcase and headed down the hallway. She poked her head in Lieutenant Figueroa's office. "LT, I'm going to Ivan's in Hollywood to ask some questions about the Russian Doll case."

Lieutenant Figueroa glanced up from his laptop. "Your partner got your back?"

"H-he had a family emergency." She smacked the doorjamb. "I got this. Just a few questions about Natalya and Austin, see if anyone knew them. The Russian community is close out there."

"Go get 'em, Falco. You're doing a good job on this case."

"Thanks, LT." As she jogged down the stairs, she puffed out her chest a little. After Austin had been murdered prior to his meeting with her and the explosion at his storage facility in San Pedro, the brass knew this was more than a domestic. She didn't want the lieutenant to regret assigning this case to her.

She placed her laptop in the trunk of her police sedan and draped her jacket on the front seat over her purse. Before she started the engine, she checked her phone and saw a text from Tim. He'd sent the cigarette butt out for DNA testing, but didn't have much else. He wasn't able to locate Azra Balik.

She snorted. It was not like he could do a find-my-phone for selected snipers.

She tapped his number and he picked up immediately. "You got my text?"

"I did. How exactly do you go about locating a sniper for hire?"

He lowered his voice to a whisper. "I have my sources. Are you and Carter on your way to Ivan's?"

Did he need to know Damon had bailed and she was heading out there alone? "He's meeting me there. I have the pieces from Austin's storage unit. Maybe someone will recognize something…like you recognized Lana's cross."

"Maybe they will, but you won't get anything from Ivan. He's a company man who toes the line. In exchange, Bratva offers him protection and an endless supply of workers from Ukraine and Russia."

"Hmm, maybe ICE can do a little investigation of those workers to find out their immigration status—or maybe I can use that to coerce information out of Ivan. It would be a shame if he lost all his staff at the same time and actually had to pay taxes and benefits for his workers."

"Don't bluff if you're not willing to follow through. A guy like Ivan can smell a con a mile away."

"Don't worry, Agent Ruskin. I'll handle this on my own."

"You mean, you and Carter."

"Yeah." She drilled her knuckle against the start button, and her engine growled to life. "I'd better get going. I'll fill you in later."

"Dinner?"

"I'll take it under advisement." She ended the call and wheeled out of the parking lot.

Traffic slowed her journey and she wouldn't make it right at opening, but the restaurant should still be quiet enough so that she wasn't competing with customers for the owner's time.

By the time she arrived at the restaurant on Sunset, only a few cars occupied the small parking lot on the side of the building. She made a hard right into the lot, which slanted uphill, and nabbed a space made for a car smaller than her sedan. Maybe she'd be out of here before the dinner crowd descended on the restaurant.

She shook out her gray jacket and slipped her arms in the sleeves. The heels of her black suede pumps crunched the gravel of the parking lot as she picked her way downhill to the sidewalk.

A patio fronted the restaurant, a low white fence separating it from the sidewalk, which was beginning to wake up with pedestrians off work in search of a cocktail or an early dinner.

Before she swept through the front door, she glanced up at the balcony jutting out from the second story, twinkling with fairy lights in the purple dusk. Must be part of the bar upstairs.

A hostess scurried to the lectern at the entrance when she heard the door snap shut. "Hello, do you have a reservation tonight?"

Eyeing the plush red decor and gleaming brass fixtures, Jane flipped open her badge. "I'm with the LAPD,

Detective Jane Falco. I'd like to speak to the owner, Ivan Kozlov."

The woman's eyes, already widened with black liner, grew even bigger. Her perfect English stumbled. "Okay, I get him."

She disappeared in the back of the restaurant, her blond ponytail bobbing vigorously from shoulder blade to shoulder blade, her steps cushioned by the deep carpet.

The door rattled open behind Jane, bringing in a gush of cool air that tempered the overheated atmosphere of the room. Jane stepped aside as a couple entered the restaurant, speaking Russian.

Several seconds later, the hostess strode back to her post, her cheeks red and her eyes bright. "Ivan will be right with you."

Jane nodded as the hostess turned from her to greet the couple in their native language. They were obviously regulars and scored a table at the window in the front of the restaurant, near the patio.

A man emerged from the back, his dark suit impeccable, his silver hair glinting in the muted light. His lips spread into a smile as he approached Jane, and she squared her shoulders as if ready to do battle.

He thrust out his hand and said in accented but strong English, "Welcome to Ivan's, Detective Falco."

Despite Jane's three-inch advantage over him, she felt his presence in his strong grip and weathered face. If she expected some poor immigrant pushover doing the bidding of the big, bad Bratva, she had the wrong guy. She couldn't imagine anyone pulling a fast one over on this man.

"Mr. Kozlov. I have a few questions for you regarding the murders of a couple—Russian immigrants. Is there someplace we can talk?"

His deep-set blue eyes scanned her face. "Ah, you don't recognize me, do you, Mrs. Sharp? And yet, I feel like I know you very well."

Chapter Thirteen

She snatched her hand back from his and tilted her chin to give herself even more height. What game was he playing with her? "I'm sorry. I don't recognize you, and I'm Detective Falco."

"Just a little teasing." His lips twisted into a smile. "Come sit with me and I'll refresh your memory."

The last thing she needed right now were memories of being Mrs. Sharp, but she followed Kozlov to a table near the bar and sat in the chair he pulled out for her with a flourish.

He shook a finger in her face, pairing it with a twinkle in his eye. "I should be offended, but I'm not. I did not deal with you for that party. Your husband had hired an event planner for the festivities."

She released a measured breath through her nose. He must've catered one of Aaron's many parties at the house, parties she'd ceased to care about or even attend in some cases. "Ex."

"Excuse me?" Kozlov tilted his head to one side like an inquisitive bird, but his beady eyes gleamed with cunning.

"Mr. Sharp is my ex-husband, and you're right. I had very little to do with his party planning." She pulled out a notebook and slapped it on the table between them. "But I'm sure your restaurant did a very fine job catering the event. Natalya Petrova."

If she'd hoped to shock him with the name, her ploy had fallen flat. Kozlov shook his head and crossed himself.

"I read about that poor girl murdered in her home. Such a shame." He tapped one finger on the table, which seemed to be a signal, as a tall waiter rushed to Ivan's side, stooping over the table with bated breath. Without looking at the young man, Kozlov said, "Max, bring me some tea, please. Something for you, Detective?"

"Tea is fine."

The waiter loped away, ignoring a diner trying to flag him down. Max had his priorities straight.

"So, you think all Russians in LA know each other, Detective?" Ivan spread his hands on the table in front of him, his thumbs touching.

"You didn't know Natalya…or Austin Walker?" She jumped as the bartender dropped a glass in the sink.

"I didn't know Natalya or this Austin Walker." She opened her mouth and he held up a hand. "I knew Oleg Stepanchikov, and I knew he'd never escape the sins of his father—even here in America."

"Do you believe his death was related to the Russian mob?"

"Russian mob?" Ivan's nostrils flared. "The US has many criminals, no? Do you categorize them all by nationality?"

Max returned with the tea, placing an ornately floral teapot on the table between them and two delicate, matching cups. He also positioned a creamer and a bowl of sugar cubes, silver tongs resting across the top, next to the pot.

"Allow me." Ivan hooked two blunt fingers around the handle of the teapot and poured the steaming liquid into Jane's cup. He repeated the process for himself, and then plucked up the silver tongs. "Sugar, Detective Falco?"

"I'll drink it black."

"It's quite strong." Ivan pinched a sugar cube between the tongs and dropped it into his tea. He placed three more in the cup and held up the tongs. "Taste first and let me know."

Jane held the cup to her mouth and blew on the tea, creating little waves in her cup. She sipped the brew and wrinkled her nose. "You're not kidding. I'll have a couple of those."

Ivan plunked two sugar cubes into her cup. "More?"

"I think that's fine, thank you." She stirred the sugar into the light brown liquid and took another sip. "You don't think the Russian mob is operating in LA? We have quite a few crimes that suggest otherwise."

"It's not the culprit for every crime committed against a Russian." He shrugged his shoulders, the fine material of his jacket barely creasing.

"You mentioned the sins of the father catching up to Austin... Oleg. His father betrayed the mob, and they murdered him and his whole family."

"I don't concern myself with old feuds from Mother

Russia, Detective Falco. I don't know what goes on here in that regard, and I don't know Natalya, nor have I ever met Oleg." He snapped his fingers, and the same waiter scurried to the table, even though the restaurant was beginning to fill up.

"Max, get Detective Falco some borscht in a container to go."

He was dismissing her already? "That's not necessary, but I also wanted to ask you if you know Lana Savchenko."

Max dropped his pencil and ducked under the table to retrieve it.

"Savchenko." Ivan steepled his fingers. "Ukrainian girl? The name is familiar, but I don't know. Why should I know this girl?"

"I received some information that she worked here. You do employ a lot of Russian and Ukrainian women at your restaurant, don't you?"

"That I do. I prefer staff that knows the language, the food, the culture." He waved his hands. "Look around you. We supply the whole atmosphere."

Max had popped up with his pencil and tapped it against a notepad, his face red. "Th-the borscht?"

"Please, take some home, Detective. You won't regret it."

"While Max is getting the borscht, I'd like to ask a few members of your staff about Lana. If she worked here, they might remember better than you." Jane knew when to accept defeat. She also knew when to apply pressure, and this wasn't the right time. She took another gulp of tea and pushed back her chair.

"The staff would know more than I." Ivan rose slowly, clutching his teacup. "Feel free to talk to them, Detective, and enjoy your borscht."

"Thank you." As Ivan meandered to another table to greet the patrons, Jane zeroed in on the bartender, who'd seemed to be eavesdropping on the majority of her conversation with Ivan.

She squeezed between two stools and rested her arms on the bar. "Excuse me."

"Yes?" He must've known she was coming for him next. He didn't even turn around from the beer tap when he answered her.

"Did you know a woman named Lana Savchenko who worked here a few months ago?"

He turned toward her, holding two beers, his dark eyes shifting over her shoulder. Was Ivan watching their exchange?

"Girls come and go." He placed the mugs on a tray. "Lana, maybe. I don't remember. So many Lanas, Mashas, Alinas, Olgas. Only so many names in Ukraine."

Jane tapped her phone to bring up the picture Alexei had given her of his sister. "Maybe you're better at faces."

He hunched over her phone, his hands wedged against the edge of the bar, his triceps flaring beneath his black T-shirt. "Pretty girl. Don't remember."

Jane snatched her phone back. She had a feeling none of the staff would remember Lana—Ivan would make sure of that. She did have one more play. She shook the scorched items they'd rescued from the fire onto the bar. "Do you recognize any of these pieces? Do they belong to any of the waitresses here?"

He poked at the jewelry with the tip of his finger. "I don't recognize them, but I don't pay attention to these things. Sorry."

As she gathered up the pieces, she thanked him and tried with the rest of the room. She asked the two waiters downstairs and the hostess, and they all gave the same answer. *Don't remember.*

If there was nothing nefarious about Lana's departure, why would they deny she worked here?

Without checking with Ivan, Jane climbed the stairs to the club portion of the restaurant. She'd seen a few people skirting in and out of the room upstairs via a heavy red drape.

When she reached the top of the stairs, she flicked back the drape and stepped into a red-carpeted room with a stage at the back, and another gleaming horseshoe bar on the left. Another bartender readied her domain for the opening.

The woman behind the bar glanced up, tucking a lock of blond hair behind her ear. "Not open here yet. You can have dinner downstairs."

"I'm not here for dinner or drinks, although I'm getting a borscht to go, whether I like it or not." Jane crossed the room, holding out her badge in front of her like a magic talisman—not that it had brought her much luck. "I'm Detective Falco, LAPD Homicide. Ivan said I could ask the staff a few questions about Natalya Petrova, Austin Walker…and Lana Savchenko."

The woman didn't miss a beat, polishing her glass.

"I heard about the murders of Natalya and Austin, but I didn't know them and they weren't regulars here. Doesn't mean they never came in. It seems like every Russian immigrant in Hollywood makes a pilgrimage to Ivan's. That other girl, Lana, she murdered, too?"

Jane swallowed. "No, but she may have some information about the cases. What's your name?"

"Masha."

The bartender downstairs hadn't been joking about the limited number of Ukrainian names. "I'd like to show you a picture of Lana, Masha."

Masha placed the glass on the mirrored shelf and wiped her palms on her black apron. "Okay."

Holding out her phone, Jane asked, "Does she look familiar to you? Did she ever work here?"

"I haven't seen her before. Lots of girls work here—in and out, like a big factory." Masha flicked her hair back. "I'll tell you one thing."

"What's that?" Jane raised her eyebrows as she tucked her phone in her purse.

"If that girl does know anything about those murders, she'd better watch her back."

Jane's heart thumped. "Why do you say that?"

"I'd think any witness to a murder would have to be careful." Masha tugged off her apron. "I'll get your borscht from the kitchen. Ivan is very proud of that soup."

Jane followed Masha downstairs to the now-crowded dining room. Masha turned at the bottom and said, "You can wait here."

Jane's gaze flicked from table to table, resting on

Ivan schmoozing with another table of diners. He certainly owned the room.

As if feeling her eyes on him, Ivan tilted his head to the side and nodded at her, smug in the knowledge that none of his staff had talked to her about Lana or anything else. At least he hadn't tossed her out like he'd done to Alexei and Tim—not that she'd gotten any more information than they had.

Masha returned, carrying a plastic bag tied at the top. She handed it to Jane solemnly. "The borscht. Finish all the way to the bottom. Enjoy."

Lifting the bag in the air, Jane said, "Thanks."

She stepped outside, and the cool night air caressed her heated face. The warmth in the restaurant was oppressive, or maybe that was Ivan's presence hanging over the room like a suffocating blanket.

She walked to her car, the borscht swinging at her side. She had to admit that the smells coming from the kitchen had made her mouth water. Only the best for Aaron and his parties. She couldn't even remember a Russian-themed event, but her ex had hosted so many galas she'd lost track at the end. Figured; he'd somehow latched onto a mob-connected restaurant.

She maneuvered onto the freeway and by the time she rolled into Benedict Canyon, the soup had filled the car with its homey aroma. As she turned into her driveway, her headlights picked out Tim's sedan parked to the side.

He jumped out and waved one hand, shielding his eyes from her lights with the other. He could've called her for an update on Ivan's—but she didn't mind his presence. He had mentioned something about dinner later—and now she was prepared.

She cracked open her car door and twisted in her seat to gather her jacket, purse and soup. Before stepping out of the car, she popped her trunk and Tim circled around the back of her sedan to claim her laptop case.

Hoisting the strap over his shoulder, he said, "You're still in one piece—no bruises or broken bones."

"That's because I didn't charge in there, demanding he give up Lana." She held up the bag. "And he sent me away with borscht."

"Are you sure he didn't poison it?" He joined her on the front porch as she unlocked her door.

"If you're worried, I'll be the taste-tester. The smell of this soup all the way home has made me ravenous—poisoned or not." She nudged the door open with her hip, and Tim followed her inside.

She placed the soup on the counter and washed her hands. "Before you ask, I got nothing from Ivan or any of his staff. He knows of Natalya and Austin, but claims he didn't know them personally. Said he never saw Lana before."

"Except Alexei knows she worked at Ivan's, so Ivan is lying." He sidled next to her at the sink and she left the water on, so he could wash his own hands. "I decided to take you up on your offer of soup. That *does* smell good."

Jane removed two bowls from the cupboard and popped the lid off the disposable container. The steam rose in lazy curls, and she inhaled the savory, tangy smell.

She grabbed a ladle from the drawer and dipped it

into the liquid. "Anything you don't like? It has beets in here."

"I would expect borscht to have beets. Everything's okay." Tim held up two small containers, shaking one. "Looks like sour cream and green stuff in this one."

"I think that's dill." Jane filled the bowls, put a dollop of sour cream on the surface of each and sprinkled the dill onto the sour cream. "Authentic. I'll take these to the kitchen table and you grab a couple of spoons."

"I'll clean this up a little." He turned on the kitchen faucet and stuck the to-go container under the stream of water to rinse it.

"I'd forgotten how handy you were in the kitchen." Tim didn't respond with one of his usual smart comebacks, and Jane glanced over her shoulder.

Tim had the container turned upside down, his forehead creased, and the running water forgotten.

"What are you looking at?"

He turned off the water. "Looks like you came away from Ivan's with more than just the soup."

"What do you mean?" She jumped from her chair and barreled toward him.

He held out the container, words in black felt tip scrawled on the bottom, reciting the words that blurred before her eyes. "Get Max alone."

Chapter Fourteen

Tim's gaze shifted from the soup container to Jane's eyes, the light of excitement in them making the amber in their depths glow. "Who the hell is Max?"

"He's a waiter at Ivan's. He served me and Ivan some tea. I asked him about Lana, but he claimed ignorance."

"Because Ivan was sitting right there, watching his every move."

"Exactly." She clapped her hands. "Finally! We can question Max away from the restaurant and find out what he knows about Lana."

"Wait a second." Tim flicked the to-go container with his finger. "Who wrote this? It could've been Ivan himself setting a trap."

"I think I have an idea." Jane patted the chair next to her. "Sit down. Your soup's getting cold."

He grabbed a couple of spoons from the drawer and took the container with the secret message to the table with him. He plopped it down between them.

"Who do you think wrote that message?"

Jane plucked up the spoon and stirred the broth, sending the vegetables and meat into a whirlpool.

"Masha. She was setting up the bar in the club upstairs. Impeccable English. She answered the same as everyone else when I asked if she knew Natalya, Austin or Lana, though."

"She had a change of heart?" Tim dunked his spoon into the borscht and blew on the contents.

"Like the others, she was probably afraid Ivan would hear her, or one of his spies would hear and report her. I told her Ivan had offered me some borscht to go, and she insisted on getting it for me from the kitchen. She wrote me the message then." Jane slurped some soup from her spoon and made a satisfied noise in the back of her throat.

"It's good, isn't it?" Tim wiped his mouth with a napkin. "Why do you think Masha is helping you?"

"I don't know. Maybe she was friends with Lana. Maybe she wants to do the right thing. Maybe she's scared she's next."

"Next for what?"

Waving her spoon in the air, Jane said, "Next for whatever is going on there. The FBI is investigating a sex trafficking scheme run by Bratva. You know that. You saw where they were keeping the women in San Pedro with your own eyes. Natalya and Austin knew something about it. Lana may be a victim of it, and Ivan hires Russian and Ukrainian girls at his restaurant—fresh meat for Bratva."

"I'd say that about sums it up, but where do they keep the women before shipping them out? We got a tip on that warehouse in San Pedro, but they're not going to be dumb enough to return to the same location." He drilled his finger into the table. "And we need to nab the person at the top. If we can bring down Bratva's top dog in LA, we can put a stop to this trafficking ring."

"The FBI doesn't know who that is? How long have you been working this case?"

He lifted his shoulders. "On and off for years—not just the human trafficking, but the drugs, the money laundering, the heists. The real head of the snake is in Russia and we can't touch him, but he has his capos here. That's who we need to reach."

"Bringing down the Russian mob in LA is not my focus but if finding Natalya's and Austin's killers and discovering what happened to Lana leads to it, then I'm all in." She scraped the bottom of her bowl with her spoon. "This is so good. No wonder my ex hired them to cater one of his parties."

Tim choked on his soup, and his eyes watered. "What did you say?"

"Apparently, my ex-husband had Ivan's cater one of his parties." A small crease formed between Jane's eyebrows. "Ivan remembered that, and that was the first thing he mentioned to me."

"Did you deal with Ivan at the time?"

Jane's hand curled around her napkin at the side of her bowl. "No. Aaron threw several parties without my input at the end of our marriage. I was done by that time. I didn't even remember that he'd had a Russian-themed party."

"How do you know Ivan's telling the truth?"

"Why would he lie about something like that?" She toyed with her spoon.

"To get on your good side, establish some rapport. Your husband was someone who played fast and loose with the rules. Maybe Ivan thought you'd be like him, and he could get around you."

"I wonder…" Jane spun her phone around to face her. "Maybe I should call Aaron and ask him. I'm sure he'd remember. He has a good memory for things that are important to him."

"You're still in touch with him?" Tim ran the pad of his thumb around the rim of his bowl. "If I ever run into that guy, I'm gonna flatten him."

"Yeah, okay." Jane rolled her eyes, but her blush told a different story. "That'll be great for your career, tough guy."

Tim narrowed his eyes. "Terry would've done it in a heartbeat."

"You're not Terry anymore." She picked up her phone. "Aaron and I have called each other regarding business matters, and I think this qualifies."

As she tapped the phone, Tim hunched forward. "Let me hear what he has to say."

Aaron picked up on the second ring. "Hey, Jane. What do you need?"

"I don't *need* anything, Aaron, but I have a question for you."

"Shoot, babe."

A hot flash of anger scorched Tim's chest. How could this man treat Jane so casually after hitting her?

"Did you ever have a Russian-themed party where you hired Ivan's restaurant in Hollywood to cater it?"

"I did, yeah. I'm surprised you remembered. I hosted

it for that guy from Russia who was developing Russian TV shows for distribution here in the States. That borscht was killer."

Jane nodded. "You met the owner, Ivan?"

"Just briefly. My...ah...assistant Sloane is the one who set that up, so she dealt with everything."

Jane's lips tightened at the mention of Sloane, and Tim could only imagine what that meant. Her ex was a piece of work.

"All right. That's all I needed to know."

"That guy, Ivan?"

"Yeah?" Jane exchanged a quick glance with Tim.

"The Russian I was hosting had heard of him before. Said he was one bad dude back in Mother Russia. Was real nervous about whether or not Ivan himself would be at the party."

"Really?"

"Does that help you, Janie? 'Cuz I wanna help you."

Tim snorted, and Jane stifled a laugh. "Yeah, thanks, Aaron. Bye."

She ended the call before her ex could respond.

"That's interesting." She drummed her fingers on the table.

"What? That he still calls you babe and wants to help you?" Tim wiped his palms on the thighs of his jeans.

"He calls everyone babe. That's what they do in the business." She nestled her empty bowl inside his. "It's interesting that Aaron's Russian guest knew Ivan and apparently feared him."

"Ivan Kozlov is not someone who's been on our radar before. Up to this point, we believed he was a Russian immigrant restaurateur, bullied by Bratva into providing favors for them."

"Did Ivan seem bullied to you? He might be more involved than you thought." She picked up the bowls and scooted back from the table. "I know one way we can find out more."

"You're not going back there, are you?" Tim folded his arms. Jane already had a sniper tracking her. She didn't need to rouse Ivan's suspicions.

"Oh, we're going back there, all right, but I'm going to skip the pointless conversation with Ivan."

"Max?"

"We have a few hours before the restaurant closes. We can ambush him when he gets off work. Get him alone—as Masha suggested."

"At least you're including me." He joined her at the sink and cranked on the water.

"Of course I'm including you." She squeezed his bicep with a wet hand. "You're my muscle."

"You think you need muscle? How big is this Max?"

"Taller than you, but much, much skinnier. He may need some encouragement to spill what he knows." She bumped him with her hip. "If you've got the testosterone flowing, better to use it for a good cause instead of roughing up my ex."

Tim chuckled, but he'd faced the scary truth—he'd be willing to take on anyone in any way to protect Jane.

Two hours later, they sat in Jane's civilian car in a valet parking lot across the street from Ivan's. Jane had flashed her badge at the parking attendant, so he'd allowed them to park for free at the edge of the lot with a view of Sunset.

Jane sipped her coffee. "I hope Max is just a waiter and won't go upstairs to the club for a second shift."

"Upstairs closes at midnight. I checked on my phone, just in case." Tim shook the dregs of his own coffee. "If that's the case, I can run over to the coffee place for a couple of refills."

"I'm wired enough. I can't take anymore." She grabbed his thigh. "Look. The lights are off on the patio. The restaurant is closing."

"And there's the first escapee." Tim jabbed his finger at the windshield as a waitress slipped out the side door and stood on the curb.

A few minutes later, a beat-up car rolled up in front of the restaurant and she jumped inside.

Jane blew out a breath. "At least it looks like some of the waiters don't do double duty."

When the side door swung open again, Jane poked his arm. "That's him. That's Max."

Tim squinted, picking out the figure of a man between the traffic on the street. The young man shoved his hands in his pockets and stepped off the curb into the crosswalk.

"Looks like he's coming our way." Tim punched the ignition button on Jane's Mercedes, which she'd allowed him to drive. The German engine growled to life, and he waved out the window to the parking attendant.

He crawled across the lot to the exit. Max had already crossed the street and waited at the corner for the light to change.

Jane said, "If he's walking up Sunset, we can roll up on him. Maybe he parked his car on a side street."

"We should try to get him in the car here instead of following him in his vehicle."

"Agreed." Jane scooted forward in her seat and powered down her window.

Tim idled at the lot's exit, waiting for Max to make his move so that he could follow him on the street.

With a gap in the traffic, Tim glanced to his left at Ivan's just to make sure nobody was watching Max. This could still be a setup.

His heart stuttered in his chest when he spotted a stocky African-American man loitering in front of Ivan's. "Jane?"

"Yeah? We can't move yet, or we'll be forced to get ahead of him. Wait until he crosses."

"Jane, isn't that your partner at Ivan's? Carter?"

"What?" She swiveled her head around and gasped. "Wh-what's he doing here? Did he get the time mixed up? I told him five o'clock and he canceled on me."

A petite brunette burst out of the side door of the restaurant and jumped into Damon's arms.

As Jane's eyes widened, Tim said, "Looks like he didn't cancel on her."

Chapter Fifteen

Jane's heart pounded. Why didn't her partner tell her he knew all about Ivan's…and knew someone who worked there? Was that why he didn't want to go the restaurant with her when she questioned Ivan?

"What are you going to do? Confront him now?" Tim jerked his thumb to the side. "Our quarry is making his move."

"Go after Max. I'll deal with Damon later. I don't understand why he didn't tell me he knew someone at Ivan's."

Tim put the car in gear and rolled onto the street, turning left toward Sunset. "Who says she works there? Maybe he's meeting a date there? Maybe you gave him the idea."

"A date coming out of that side door?" She made a shooing motion with her fingers. "Pull up a little. There's nobody behind us. We can give Max a little head start."

Max walked with his loping gait about halfway up the block and stopped at a bus stop.

Tim breathed out. "Perfect. He's taking the bus. We'll offer him a ride."

"And if he doesn't get in?"

Tim flexed his muscles. "That's what I'm here for, remember?"

Jane licked her lips as Tim turned the corner, her brain still fuzzy from Damon's presence at Ivan's. What would he say if she just asked him point-blank? Would he lie?

Tim interrupted her thoughts. "Aaand he's at the bus stop. How can he refuse a ride from us?"

Tim hugged the curb, cruising toward the bus zone.

Max, staring at his phone, hadn't even noticed.

Jane leaned out the window. "Hey, Max. Remember me?"

His head jerked up, and his eyes bugged out. That and his long neck gave him the appearance of a startled insect. And she didn't want him flying away.

"Detective Falco. You served me some tea at Ivan's when I was talking to your boss."

"Y-yes." His eyes darted down the street toward the restaurant, as if he thought Ivan could see him now.

"I just want to ask you a few more questions." She patted the side of the car. "Hop in."

Tim popped the locks. "Comfortable, heated leather seats or the smelly bus. The choice is yours, Max."

As he glanced past her at Tim, Max swallowed, his Adam's apple looking like a golf ball in his skinny neck. "Am I under arrest?"

Tim's invitation must've sounded more threatening than he'd intended—or maybe not.

"Arrest?" Jane laughed. "Of course not. I just want

to talk—away from the restaurant. Oh, and thanks for ordering that borscht for me. Out of this world."

"Get in the car, Max." Tim flashed his teeth. "I see the bus in my rearview mirror, and the driver's not gonna be too happy with me in his spot."

Max took a jerky step toward the car, his long legs almost tangling. He pulled open the door to the back seat, and the leather creaked as he slid inside.

Tim adjusted the rearview mirror. "Seat belt. We don't wanna break the law with a cop in the car."

It took Max three tries to tug the seat belt across his body and snap it into place.

Tim pulled into the traffic of Sunset, seamlessly blending into the flow. "You hungry, Max, or do you eat at the restaurant? Coffee? Something else to drink?"

"I…um, usually get a burger when I get off work."

Tim said, "Burgers and fries, it is."

"N-not here." Max twisted in his seat to look out the back window.

Jane almost felt sorry for the kid, and Tim wasn't helping matters with his jovial yet slightly sinister manner. It was like he had another shoe to drop, keeping Max on edge. She had a feeling Max might be more receptive to a gentle touch. The kid wouldn't be able to put a coherent sentence together if Tim terrified him too much.

She turned in her seat and smiled over her shoulder. "No problem. Where do you live, Max? We'll take you anywhere you want to go on the way home."

Max's eye twitched but he was able to answer without stuttering this time. "I live in Reseda. There's a burger joint on Ventura I like."

"Ventura Boulevard, here we come." Tim flicked on the turn signal. "That's a long bus ride. Aren't you glad we picked you up?"

Max gripped the armrest, not quite sure which would be worse, the long bus ride or facing Tim's questions. He puffed out a breath and sank against the leather. "I guess."

"Perfect." Jane pulled out her phone. "Tell us which burger place, and I'll put it in my GPS."

Max gave her the name of a dive burger joint on Ventura, and she entered it in her phone. Pinching Tim's thigh, she asked, "Are you Russian, Max? Your English is very good."

"Yeah, I came here when I was a little kid. I'm taking classes at Pierce College—computer classes."

She nodded encouragingly. "Good for you. Do your parents live in LA?"

"My parents?" He shot forward in his seat, grabbed the back of her headrest. "Why are you asking about my parents?"

"Just making small talk, Max. Nobody's going to contact your parents."

"They live in New York." He wiped the back of his hand across his forehead. "They run a dance studio."

"Do you dance?" She turned her head to the side so Max could see her face, and caught Tim rolling his eyes. Mr. FBI could scoff all he wanted, but at least the conversation had calmed Max somewhat and he wasn't a jittering ball of nerves.

Max snorted. "I had to learn, but I hated it. My parents gave up on me."

"Better future in computers than dancing." The sound of Tim's voice made Max jump again. Even Tim's approval couldn't win over Max. It was a good thing Jane hadn't told Max that Tim was FBI.

She allowed Max to sit in silence the rest of the way to the diner. He'd need to think carefully about what he wanted to say. If he knew something about women being trafficked and stayed silent, she'd make sure he understood that he was complicit in their misery. If he feared for his safety, maybe Tim could get the FBI to offer him some protection.

Tim located the burger place and snagged a metered parking spot on the street. "This is where you go?"

"Yeah, they're good…and cheap."

"Meal's on us, Max—if, you know, you can help us out."

Jane slugged Tim's arm. "It's on us anyway, Max, but we sure hope you can give us some information about Ivan."

At the mention of Ivan's name, Max's face blanched first and then color rushed into his cheeks. He jumped from the car so fast when Tim parked that Jane thought for a minute he was making a run for it. But he waited for them on the sidewalk, his Gumby arms wrapped around his lanky body.

They followed him into the restaurant, and Tim gave

Max two twenties. "Order your regular, and get me a Coke and some fries. Jane?"

"Diet Coke for me. I might as well stay up the rest of the night."

Tim claimed a table by the window, the few customers occupying the restaurant too busy with their food to notice them.

They sat side by side, leaving the seat across from them for Max.

Tim plucked some napkins from the dispenser. "Why were you pinching me in the car?"

"You're too gruff with Max. He's on edge. He's not going to cooperate if he can't think straight."

"Gruff?" Tim tapped his chest. "I offered him food and told him ditching dancing for computers was a good move."

"Don't play dumb with me." She pinched him again for good measure. "You come across like a sinister executioner offering him a last meal."

"That's a good one." He pinched her back, but on the inside of her thigh, making her shiver. "Not the right touch, huh?"

His touch would always be right for her. She fluttered her lashes. "No. Let me ask the questions."

"You got it." He bumped her shoulder as if they were coconspirators.

Max approached their table, carrying three drinks bunched together in his hands, in true waiter fashion. He set them down, dropping three straws in the middle.

"I'm gonna wait for the food at the counter." He jerked his thumb over his shoulder.

As Max walked away, stuffing his straw in his cup, Tim said, "He doesn't want to spend one more minute with us than he has to."

"Obviously, which means he has something to share." Jane peeled the paper from her straw and shoved it into the plastic lid.

Tim had sucked down his drink and was ready for a refill by the time Max returned with the food. Max put down a plastic basket with a large double burger crowding out a massive helping of fries, pushing a few over the edge. He placed a second basket with even more fries in front of Tim.

Next to the fries, Max slapped down a crumpled ten, some ones and change.

"You weren't kidding. What a deal." Tim swept the money into his palm.

Jane picked at a few of Tim's fries and slurped her own drink before taking a deep breath. "Max, we have reason to believe you know something about Ivan's operations out of the restaurant."

Indicating he knew this was coming, Max didn't even miss a bite. He chewed, his lean jaw working rhythmically as he studied the ceiling.

"Who told you that?"

"Not important. Is it true?"

"Stuff happens there, but nobody tells me about it."

"I'm sure they don't." Jane brushed her fingers together, dislodging the salt onto a napkin. "Nobody is accusing you of doing anything illegal or being involved in illegal activity, but you know something…don't you?"

"I'm just a waiter. Ivan barely knows my name." He swiped some grease from his chin with a napkin.

"We know Lana worked at Ivan's. Did you know her?"

Max screwed up his eyes. "Lana…"

Tim slammed his fist on the table, making the fries jump and the ice tinkle. "Cut the crap, Max. You know Lana."

Max clutched at his chest, his face crumpling. He let out a sob. "Lana was my…friend."

Tim kicked her under the table. Okay, the hardline had wrenched the truth from Max.

Jane shoved a napkin toward Max and his runny nose and leaking eyes. "I'm sorry, Max, and now she's missing."

Max mopped his face with the napkin and blew his nose. "She wouldn't just take off like that. She wouldn't just leave without saying goodbye."

"Was Ivan or anyone else harassing her before she disappeared?"

His chin dropped to his chest. "Natalya Petrova."

Jane brought her hands together under the table, clasping them between her knees. "The murdered woman?"

"Yeah, that's her." He picked some soggy lettuce from his burger and flicked it on to the table. "When I heard she was killed… I was happy. And I'm not sorry about it."

Tim stuffed a french fry in his mouth, as if this weren't completely unexpected news. "You were happy

Natalya was murdered because she'd been harassing Lana?"

"Yes."

"Did you kill Natalya because she'd been harassing Lana?"

"No!"

Jane put her hand on Tim's arm. "What was Natalya doing to harass Lana?"

"Trying to get her to work for her." Max slumped in his chair.

"In what capacity?" Jane held her breath as Max sat up. He wiped his face and took a sip of his soda.

He toyed with his straw for a second. "Turning tricks."

This time, Jane couldn't hide her surprise, and her mouth dropped open. "Natalya was running some kind of prostitution ring?"

"She was trying." Max wagged his finger. "Oh, she'd correct you and tell you it wasn't prostitution. She was developing an escort service. She wanted to employ only the best-looking women, and she promised to hook them up with wealthy men."

Jane rubbed the back of her neck and glanced at Tim. How'd they miss this about Natalya? They'd been so focused on her as a victim, which she was, that they'd looked past the possibility that she could also have been a victimizer.

As Jane seemed to have lost her ability to speak, Tim picked up the slack. "What about Austin Walker? Was he involved in Natalya's…escort service?"

"She wanted him to be. She knew about Austin's background before she started dating him, for sure.

She used him, figured he'd have connections she could tap into." Max hunched his skinny shoulders. "She was playing with fire."

"How so?" Tim asked.

Max blinked as if Tim had just asked the world's dumbest question. "Because she was stepping into Ivan Kozlov's territory, that's why."

"Wait, wait." Jane waved her hands over the table. "*Ivan's* territory? I thought he was just the restaurant guy who facilitated things for Bratva."

"That's what he wants everyone to think. He's connected to Bratva, but he's a boss. He runs the girls."

Jane's hand moved to her throat. "So Natalya was in direct competition with Ivan?"

"Sort of. Ivan traffics women, sells them on the market. Natalya wasn't interested in any of that. She wanted to run some high-class call girl ring—with Austin's help. It's just that they were going after the same women—like Lana." Max hung his head again and sniffled.

Tim pointed a fry at Max. "How do you know all this? Like you said, you're just a waiter at Ivan's and the boss barely knows your name."

"I told you. Lana and I had a thing, or at least I had a thing for Lana." He gave a crooked, watery smile. "She was outta my league, but we were friends."

"And she divulged all this information to you? Information about Natalya and Austin and Ivan?"

Tim cut her off brusquely. "What's Lana's sister's name?"

"Sister?" Max dragged the back of his hand across

his nose. "She never talked about a sister, but she has a brother named Alexei. He was some hotshot military guy or something. She always told me he would get her out of any jam. I guess not this time."

"Does Ivan know about you and Lana?" Jane narrowed her eyes as Max shook his head so hard his hair whipped back and forth. "Why do you think someone would clue us in that you had some dirt on the restaurant?"

"It wasn't Ivan." Max pulled his basket with the rest of his food toward him. "A few of the girls there knew about me and Lana—knew we were friends. I guess knew I had a big-time crush on her."

Tim hunched forward, his forearms on either side of his empty basket of fries. "Were you upset that your big-time crush on Lana wasn't reciprocated?"

"What? No." Max turned to Jane. "Why does he always have to go there?"

She lifted her shoulders, nudging Tim with her elbow. Her cop instincts told her this kid had nothing to do with Lana's disappearance. "When was the last time you saw Lana, and what were the circumstances?"

"Last time I saw her was about a month ago at work. We both had a shift on the same night, but I was in the restaurant and she was upstairs in the club. Asked her if she wanted to go hiking with me in Griffith Park that weekend, and she said she'd text me. She hadn't been feeling well. I never heard from her again. Her phone went dead." He stuffed the rest of his burger in his mouth. "Is that it? I need to go home."

"Just one more thing." Jane held up her finger and

pulled out her phone. She scrolled to a picture of Damon at his desk in Robbery-Homicide. "Have you ever seen this man before?"

Max took a quick glance at the picture and grabbed several napkins from the dispenser. "I know him. He works for Ivan."

Chapter Sixteen

Jane's stomach did a somersault, and it had nothing to do with the greasy fries she had just eaten. "No, you're mistaken. Take another look."

"I don't have to." Max balled up the napkins between his hands. "That's DC. He dates one of the women upstairs and meets with Ivan privately."

Jane could feel the blood draining from her face, and Tim snatched the phone from her hand.

"Look again, Max. This guy is DC?"

Max sighed and dropped the napkins in his basket, but he leaned forward and zoomed in on Damon's face, using his sticky fingers to get a close-up. "That's DC. He goes out with Sissy."

"Sissy?" Jane sawed her bottom lip with her teeth. Had Damon ever told her the name of his girlfriend? She'd just assumed the picture of the cute African-American woman on his desk was his girlfriend. "Is she Russian or Ukrainian?"

"Oh, she's Russian. Her name's Anastasia, but she goes by Sissy."

Tim snatched the phone back and wiped the screen

with his sleeve before handing it back to her. "You're assuming DC works for Ivan because he meets with him, but you don't know what the meetings are about, do you?"

"No, but he goes into Ivan's private office sometimes, so I'm pretty sure he's doing business in there."

"D-do you know what DC does when he's not working for Ivan?" Jane stuffed her hands beneath her thighs. Could Damon be doing some undercover work for Vice?

"I don't know. He's just a guy." Max braced his hands on the edge of the table. "Can I go now? I've got class tomorrow. That's all I know. I swear."

Jane took a long drink of her soda. Max knew more than he realized...more than they had realized.

Tim answered him. "Sure, but we might need to talk to you again, so don't take off. You want a ride?"

"I'm a few blocks from here. I walk it all the time. Thanks for the meal."

Max had left the diner and made it out of their eyesight before Jane met Tim's eyes. "What the hell is Damon up to?"

Tim nestled Max's basket into his. "Could he be undercover?"

"And nobody told me?"

"If everyone knew about his role, it wouldn't be undercover then, would it?"

"Yeah, but with Natalya's murder possibly linked to the Russian mob and Damon working that case, wouldn't you think it would come up?"

"I don't know how undercover assignments work for

LAPD—" Tim spread his hands "—but for us, once you're undercover nobody knows."

"Yeah, I remember." She shook the ice in her cup. "He has a Russian girlfriend, though."

"Sometimes undercover requires a girlfriend." He lifted one shoulder.

"Yeah, I remember that, too." She pushed her cup away. "I can't believe he wouldn't tell me. His being at Ivan's is crucial to this investigation. It explains why he didn't come with me to the restaurant tonight. What else does it explain?"

"You can't ask him. We're going to have to do some undercover for ourselves, and our first stop is Sissy."

"She'll run right to Damon."

Tapping the side of his head, Tim said, "Not if we tell her we're gonna rat her out to Ivan for sleeping with a cop."

She grabbed Tim's wrist. "What if she already knows that, Tim? What if Damon is working for Ivan in his capacity as a detective?"

"Then your partner is dirty, Jane."

She covered her face with her hands. "And we were getting along so great. I hate the idea of sneaking behind his back. I don't have the best reputation with partners."

"That reputation is gonna get a whole lot worse if it comes out your partner is crooked. You're going to get painted with the same brush, especially if there's evidence you knew about his activities."

She rubbed her eyes with her fists, not even caring if she smeared her makeup. "One little talk with a waiter and this whole case has gone sideways. Natalya was threatening Lana? Natalya was competing with Ivan? Where does Austin fall among all these criminals? Did he tell Alexei about Natalya? Why'd he reach out to me? Why did he have a storage container with women's jewelry and God knows what else?"

Tim had held up his hands and started counting her questions on his fingers but gave up. "We start with one thing at a time. Let's investigate Natalya first. See how far she got in her business venture and if she might've harmed Lana. The other possibility is that Lana agreed to work for Natalya and Ivan had both of them killed."

Jane rubbed her arms. "And my partner? What do I do about Damon? I don't want to go to the lieutenant. What if I'm completely off base? What if Max is completely off base? I'll look like a fool and like I'm trying to sabotage Damon's career. I can't go down that road."

"You said Damon was new. Where'd he come from?"

"Vice, Northeast Division."

"Start there. You know someone in Vice who's discreet?"

"Yes, I think so."

"Maybe this is a case leftover from Vice. Take it slow."

She released a long breath. "Okay, and maybe you can use some of your own undercover skills."

"In what way?"

"If we come at Sissy like a couple of cops, she's going to blab to her boo, Damon, right away. But a good-looking hunk of man like you? You might be able to wheedle some information out of her."

"I can't go back to the club." Tim crossed one finger

over the other. "I'm not welcome there, and Ivan would have me figured out in two seconds."

"You could watch her. See where she goes. Maybe you could run into her somewhere else." She dug her fingers into her hair. "I don't have to tell you how to do it."

"I can't believe you're encouraging me to go covert on some other unsuspecting woman."

"I hope this is a little different. You're not going to actually sleep with Sissy."

He brushed her hair from her neck and whispered in her ear. "There's only one woman I want to sleep with."

She jerked back, but her skin buzzed where his fingers lightly rested. "We're sitting here talking about a million unresolved threads, and you're thinking about sex?"

"Yeah." His dark eyes twinkled.

"Then why are we still sitting in this dump?" She smacked her cup on the table and pushed out of her chair, almost knocking it over.

Tim's eyebrows jumped, and then a smile spread across his face. "Do we need to leave a tip? I'm feeling generous all of a sudden."

"Go for it." She grabbed the edges of his jacket and planted a hard kiss on his mouth.

Tim dropped a few bucks on the table and grabbed her hand, leading her out of the diner. His fingers laced through hers, as if he were afraid she'd change her mind and take off. Not a chance. This had been building up between them for too long to stop it now.

She didn't know if the danger and excitement of

working a complex case had her blood singing or if it was being with Tim again, but she'd never felt more alive—not since her fling with Terry Rush.

She had to grab this opportunity with both hands—forget her parents' abusive relationship, forget her own failed marriage. If Tim could let go of his past, she could do the same.

They hit the sidewalk, and Tim pulled her around the corner of the building. He pushed her up against the uneven stucco and pressed his lips against hers.

Jane slid her leg between his thighs, weaving her fingers into his thick hair. As she dug her nails into his scalp, she sucked his tongue into her mouth.

They clung together like two people drowning in a sea of regrets and pent-up longing. Her bones felt like liquid as the heat from Tim's kiss coursed through her body. She just knew that if she released the grip she had on his belt in the back, she'd slide down the wall.

Someone shouted down the street, and they sprang apart. Jane blinked, forgetting for a few seconds where they were.

Tim lightly wrapped his fingers around her wrist. "I know Benedict Canyon seems far, far away right now, but we should at least get out of the street. Max doesn't live in the best area of Reseda."

She traced the butt of his gun in his jacket pocket. "We're both strapped."

He rolled his eyes. "When I'm kissing you, someone could literally come up behind me, take the weapon out of my pocket and hold it to my temple and I wouldn't notice."

"Then we'd better find a safer place to make out." Tugging on his hand, she gave a little skip.

As they walked to her car, Tim kept throwing glances her way, squeezing her hand. When they reached the Mercedes, he brought her hand to his lips and imprinted a kiss on the back of it. "You're sure about this?"

"Don't kill the vibe." She shoved him toward the passenger side. "I'll drive. I know this area better than you do."

He saluted. "Yes, ma'am."

He opened the driver's-side door for her first, and then slid into the passenger seat. "Where are we going? Back to your place?"

"Shh." She put her finger on his lips.

He kissed the tip and said, "Okay, you're in charge, Detective Falco. I'm all yours."

"You're not all mine, yet—" she ran a knuckle from his knee, up his thigh, to his crotch "—but you soon will be."

Tim made an exaggerated gulping sound and shrugged out of his jacket. He placed it carefully in the back seat, his weapon still weighing down his pocket.

Then she got down to business. "Freeway first. Shouldn't be too crowded this time of night, but you never know."

Jane headed south and then took the 101, which slowed to a crawl almost immediately. She swore. "Just when you need to get someplace fast."

"At least we're not in the middle of the street any-more." Tim squeezed her bare knee and then slid his hand up her thigh. His finger tickled the edge of her underwear, and she squirmed in her seat.

Clutching the steering wheel, she muttered through gritted teeth. "Are you trying to make me crash?"

He clicked his tongue. "You're the one who lit this fire. You can't stop the conflagration now."

"Who said I wanted to?" She clamped her thighs together, trapping his hand.

His grin couldn't get any bigger. "I thought you were the cautious type."

"Where has that ever gotten me?" She took the turn-off for Beverly Glen Boulevard, and traffic eased up. It still wasn't going fast enough for what she had in mind.

As they got closer to Mulholland, the cars thinned out and the road started to wind through the mountains. Tim's fingers kept teasing her, ramping up her desire. She clamped harder on the steering wheel to keep the car on the road, which only increased the sexual tension sizzling between them.

When she couldn't take it anymore, she careened off the road and pulled into the Stone Canyon Overlook. She threw the car into Park, her fingers scrabbling to release her seat belt. She scrambled over the center console and straddled him, her skirt hiking up her thighs.

Hooking his hands around her waist, he said, "Are you sure you don't want to enjoy this view first? Isn't that the Stone Canyon Reservoir down there?"

She smacked his hip with her palm. "Terry would've never been admiring the view with me in his lap."

"Oh, you want Terry back, do you?" He reclined his seat, pulling her with him.

While he lifted his hips, Jane undid his jeans and yanked them down his muscular thighs, the hair on his legs tickling her smooth skin.

He reached up to pull off her panties but after some awkward maneuvering on her part and a few curses on his, he ripped them off. The action sent a shiver of pleasure down her spine.

As he pulled her head toward him for a kiss, he slid his hand between her legs. "Now that we don't have to worry about crashing the car, I'll finish what I started."

She rested her head on his chest, while his fingers made lazy circles toward her throbbing flesh. He stroked her, and she moved her hips to the rhythm of his touch.

Her breath sounded harsh in the confines of the car, and the windows fogged up with the evidence of their passion. She rocked against his invasion of all her senses, her thighs clamping his hips, her muscles coiling.

When her release came, she arched her back and gasped, his name on her lips.

His voice raspy, he whispered, "Guide me inside you."

Still trembling with her climax, she reached down where their bodies met and stroked his erection. He groaned, his pelvis jutting forward. Raising her body and bracing on her knees, she placed his head at her opening. Then she sank down upon him, sheathing him to his hilt with her wet embrace.

Tim let out a long breath that turned into a whistle.

Cupping her breast over her blouse, he said, "Come back here and kiss me."

She leaned forward as much as she could without losing their connection and nibbled his bottom lip before drawing it into her mouth. He grunted against her lips and slipped both hands beneath her skirt. He dug his fingers into the soft flesh of her derriere, guiding her movement against him.

She rode him as she toyed with his tongue, sucking it in and out of her mouth to the tempo he set with his thrusts. He lifted his backside from the seat of the car, plunging into her with a deep need, as if he couldn't go far enough.

He stilled for a second, his body completely rigid, and then he emitted a low, guttural sound from his throat as he exploded inside her. He growled, "Open your eyes."

Until she'd heard his command, she hadn't realized she'd closed her eyes, reveling in each tactile sensation. Her lids flew open and she met his dark, burning gaze as he spent himself into her core.

His body relaxed, and he pinched her chin between his fingers. He pressed his lips against hers, and she tasted the salt from the beads of sweat crawling down his face.

Cupping his face with her hands, she said, "Did we just have sex in a car like a couple of teenagers?"

"At least it's a Mercedes instead of a beat-up Chevy." He shifted beneath her, and her toes curled, still secure in her low-heeled pumps. She could spend the night with him in this car and die a happy woman.

Lights from the road beyond their turnout came into focus, and she blinked. Had they taken the make-out spot of some actual teenagers? She tugged on Tim's earlobe. "I think we have company."

His frame stiffened. "What do you mean?"

"A car turned off the road. This is a popular spot for a rendezvous." She squinted as the headlights grew brighter, lining up behind her car.

The oncoming vehicle illuminated the inside of her car, and Tim twisted in his seat, dislodging her from his lap. "That's a truck."

The driver of the truck revved the engine, and Jane's stomach dropped. She clawed at the steering wheel to pull herself back into the driver's seat and off Tim's lap.

"Get down, Jane!" Tim dove over the console, reaching into the back seat for his jacket.

Just as Jane scrambled into her seat, the truck roared, its lights flooding their interior. Then it slammed into the back of her car...and propelled them through the guardrail and into the ravine below.

Chapter Seventeen

The force of the crash threw Tim toward the dashboard, but he clutched at his jacket, dragging it with him into the front seat. Jane's car rolled down the hill toward the view he'd barely noticed before, bumping and crackling over rocks and underbrush, the smell of burning rubber scorching his nostrils.

As his shoulder hit the dash, he flung out his arm to stop Jane's body from smacking into the steering wheel. All he got was a handful of her blouse as she screamed.

He held his breath while the car continued its agonizing journey down the hill. If nothing stopped it, they'd end up tipping into the canyon...unless they jumped first. When he glanced out the window, he realized his mind was working in slow motion, but the car was hurtling forward in real time.

"Jane, can you jump out? We gotta jump out."

She answered by shoving open her door. He waited until he saw her throw herself through the gap before bursting open his own door. His body smacked the ground, and he rolled a few feet, a bush jabbing into his ribs and stopping his downward progress.

He twisted around, his legs still hampered by his damned jeans ensnaring his thighs, and called out. "Jane! Jane, are you all right?"

She coughed from somewhere in the darkness. "Shh. They're still up there. I can see their silhouettes."

If she were talking and coherent, she must be somewhat okay.

Tim hugged his jacket to his chest, the reassuring bulk of his gun digging into his breastbone. He fumbled for the pocket of his jacket and yanked his weapon free. If their attackers tried to come down here to finish what they started, he'd have a surprise for them.

As he rubbed the dirt from his eyes, a blast from the canyon rocked the ground, sending a plume of black smoke into the night sky. Shouting from up on the ridge had Tim draw his knees to his chest and stay very still, the gun still clutched in his hand.

He wished he could see Jane, make sure she was all right. He heard nothing more from her and hoped to God that meant she was keeping quiet, so the men scouting for them would believe they went over in the car and died in that fiery explosion.

Over the crackling of the inferno in the canyon, Tim's ears picked up the sound of the low rumble of an engine. Were they leaving? Were they satisfied? Or were they taking off before the explosion and fire caught the attention of other motorists?

He uncurled his stiff fingers from the handle of his gun and dragged his pants up, grateful he wouldn't be found dead in a car with his jeans and underwear around his ankles. He staggered to his feet. "Jane? They left. Where are you, sweetheart?"

She gave a sob and crawled out from behind a bush, her figure taking shape in the smoky air. "A-are you hurt, Tim?"

"Bruised and banged up, but nothing broken. You?" he said as he limped toward her.

On her hands and knees, she raised her head at his approach. Her hair streamed down on either side of her face, and a rivulet of blood ran down her cheek.

Tim lunged forward, still unsteady on his feet, and dropped to his knees. He touched her face, tracing the source of the blood to a small cut over her eyebrow. Then he pulled her into his arms and held her close, as their hearts banged against each other's.

A beam of light crawled down the hillside, sweeping over them and Tim froze, hugging Jane tighter, willing her to melt into him and disappear. Had he been wrong about the truck leaving the scene?

A voice called out. "Is anyone down there?"

Jane twitched in his arms. "I think that's help. I'm sure the truck left."

"Do you want to take that chance? What if the truck drove off for show, while leaving one of our assailants behind to lure us out?" He felt his jacket pocket and grabbed his phone. "I rescued my jacket from the back seat during the crash. Saved my gun and my cell. Did you lose your purse?"

She jerked her thumb over her shoulder. "I snagged it as soon as the truck rammed us. I have everything."

He tapped in 911 as the Good Samaritan or one of

the bad guys yelled again. He gave the operator their location.

When he ended the call, he plucked a twig from Jane's wild hair. "On their way. Did you get tossed against the steering wheel? No airbags because we were parked."

Rubbing the back of her neck, she said, "I crossed my arms over my chest so I wouldn't break a rib or puncture a lung. My forearms hurt like hell, but I think we were spared the worst of the ramming because we went over the edge pretty quickly."

"And we were spared the worst of the accident because we jumped." He pointed toward the orange glow emanating from the ravine. "Otherwise we might've been ejected from the car when it made impact down there, or stayed put and burned to death."

She shivered. "That was close. They're not playing. How do you think they found us here?"

"Maybe they followed us, or were following Max or maybe they got a tracker on your car." He smacked his forehead with the heel of his hand. "Stupid me. I didn't think to watch for a tail when we snatched up Max, or when we left the diner. Knowing Max's relationship with Lana, maybe Ivan is having him followed."

"Don't expect me to hit my forehead. I have enough injuries, but I didn't think to check for a tail, either. Couple of great detectives here."

He rubbed her back as the sound of sirens cried above them. "We had other things on our mind, didn't we?"

"That's why we shouldn't mix business with pleasure." She cupped his jaw with her palm. "Didn't you learn your lesson the last time you went down that road?"

"So you're coming to the realization that you *were* pleasure to me during that assignment, and not all work?"

She cocked her head. "What just happened in the car between us—I mean before the truck interrupted us—proved a lot. First, you'd have to be an awfully good actor to fake *that*. Second, I'm so besotted with you I don't think I'd care if you had. What does that say about me?"

"It says you're a very wise woman who recognizes a good thing when she has it." He ran his hands down her arms before sticking them up in the air and waving. "The cavalry is here."

Tim turned on his phone's flashlight and waved it over his head. The red and blue revolving lights swept across the rugged terrain, putting them in the middle of a life-size kaleidoscope.

An officer spoke through a megaphone. "Do you need help climbing the hill?"

Tim cupped his hands around his mouth and shouted back. "No!"

Turning toward Jane, he said, "You don't, do you?"

"My knees are still a little wobbly, but I can make it. I'm going to grab my purse where I left it by that bush."

"I'll get it. You stay here. You're gonna need your strength to scramble up that hill." Flicking his flashlight at the ground, he traced his way back to where Jane had landed.

He spotted her purse, swept it up and hurried to her side. "Grab my arm. You're not exactly wearing hiking boots."

"You'd be surprised what a woman can do in heels."
She kicked up a foot to inspect the bottom of her impractical hiking shoes. "I'm sorry my car exploded into flames, but I'm hoping the fire burns it all into oblivion."

"Why? For the insurance money? Believe me it's totaled whether or not it's completely destroyed."

"It's not the insurance, silly." She grabbed his arm as he took the first step of their ascent. "I don't want the first responders to find a pair of ripped panties in there."

THE FOLLOWING MORNING, Jane rolled out of bed and winced. Pain permeated every inch of her body, down to the ends of her hair. She planted her bare feet on the area rug next to her bed and studied her toes for a second.

The truck hadn't allowed her and Tim the luxury of basking in the afterglow of their lovemaking, but she'd relived every second in her head as she drifted off to sleep last night.

Had she made a mistake? She pushed to her feet and grabbed the edge of the nightstand. Nothing about their encounter had felt like a mistake. She'd never felt more at home in her life than when Tim had entered her and made her his own.

She shuffled to her bathroom and flipped the cap off the bottle of ibuprofen on the vanity. She shook two of the green gel caps in her palm and tossed them into her mouth. She cranked on the faucet and, bending over, scooped a few handfuls of water into her mouth.

Leaving her pajamas on the bathroom floor, she stepped into the shower and activated both showerheads so that the hot water pummeled her front and back at the same time. She let out a little gasp of pleasure.

The only thing that could make this better was if Tim was sharing this with her. Last night they'd decided to head to their own places. Of course, he'd been riddled with worry when he left her, but she had to keep reminding him that she was a cop and her service revolver could provide ample protection.

She and Tim had concocted a story that they had met with a possible witness in the Valley for a case they were working on, jointly, and pulled into the overlook to discuss the meeting when a truck had forced her car down the ravine. If her ravaged underwear had survived the inferno, the accident investigation team could form its own conclusions.

Tim was going to try to find Sissy today, and she planned to go into the station and poke around her partner's activities. She hoped to God Damon wasn't involved in this mess. Bad idea to get involved with anyone working in a mob-connected place. Coming from Vice, he'd had to have known Ivan's reputation.

By the time she finished her shower, got dressed and had some yogurt, her body aches had dulled. She could even twist her neck to look over her shoulder when changing lanes on the way to the station.

She might have to use that same motion to watch her back once she got there.

As she threaded her way through the desks in Robbery-Homicide, she threw a quick glance at Damon's chair—empty. She eased out a sigh and rolled her stiff shoulders. His absence would spare her the awkward conversation she'd been dreading.

She dropped her purse in her bottom drawer and scooted up to the desk. Her gaze darted to Damon's desktop. He'd removed the picture of him and his *girl-friend*. Was he playing the field with two women? Nothing wrong with that—the guy was single, but dating a waitress at Ivan's put him in the danger zone.

With Damon gone, she'd take the opportunity to look into his work background. She'd thought of asking Trevor in Vice, but she needed to keep this hush-hush. She accessed the personnel database and entered Damon's name. There was only so much you could discover from someone's files. She certainly didn't want everyone in the department to be able to nose around her personal life with her ex.

She scrolled through his stellar career in Vice. He'd been a rock star there. He'd busted a lot of drug dealers and disrupted several rings. No surprise the brass had bumped him to Homicide. Leaning in close to the monitor, she ran a finger down the names of his arrests—no Russians in a city that boasted a healthy number of Russian gangs dealing drugs.

A smack on Damon's desk had her jumping out of her seat and her heart pounding as she clicked her mouse on a different tab.

Billy Crouch grinned at her. "Didn't mean to scare you. Heard you had a rough night last night."

She sat back in her chair, rubbing the back of her neck. "Truck pushed my car into the ravine."

"That sweet Mercedes you drive?" He clicked his tongue.

"One and the same, but thanks for asking after my health and well-being, Billy." She reached for her purse to pop a few more ibuprofen.

"I'd already heard you and that Fibbie came out of it alive." Crossing his arms, he wedged a hip against Damon's desk. "You think it's the Russians?"

"I'd just been to Ivan's asking questions, so most likely. We didn't get a license plate or even a make and model of the truck. One witness saw a truck peel out of the overlook, but it's so dark up there and he'd turned off his lights. The witness didn't get anything."

"Those bastards play rough. They figure if there's too much heat, they can hightail it back to Russia."

"I'll find them." She shifted her gaze to the empty spot on Damon's desk and asked, "Did Damon and his girlfriend break up or something?"

Billy quirked an eyebrow. "Do I look like the department gossip?"

She pointed at the area to the right of his hip. "He used to have that nice picture of the two of them, and now it's gone. Just trying to be a concerned partner."

Billy ducked his head. "That picture? That wasn't Damon's girlfriend. That's his sister."

Chapter Eighteen

Her heart flip-flopped. Had Damon lied to her about that picture, or had she just assumed? Why hide the picture now? Had he stashed it away when he found out they were going to Ivan's?

Billy said, "We...uh...had a talk about sisters one day."

She looked back at her computer screen. Everyone knew Billy's sister had been missing for years.

Shrugging, she said, "I guess I just figured that was the girlfriend he talks about all the time."

"You'd think he'd learn." Billy stood up and brushed off his slacks. "He's just coming out of a divorce. You need to give that stuff time."

Jane studied Billy's face for the hint of a smile. Billy had a rep for dating multiple women after his separation from his wife, but he hadn't gotten serious with one, yet.

Raising his hands, he said, "I'm not saying you can't date. God knows I have, but you're never ready for that special someone until you're ready. Know what I mean?"

"Yeah, I do."

"Glad you're not hurt, Falco." He tapped a long finger on her desk and walked away.

Had she given herself enough time after her marriage had ended before jumping into a relationship with Tim's undercover persona Terry? Maybe that's why she'd been so hurt when she discovered Tim was an FBI agent working her case. Her feelings had still been raw after what she'd gone through with Aaron. Was that why it felt so right this time? Was she ready?

Hunching forward, she clicked back onto the personnel website. Maybe Damon had been ready.

He'd been complaining to her about money before. Had Ivan paid him off in arrests that would boost his career instead of cash? It would've been easy and advantageous for Ivan to set up his enemies for Damon, serve them to him on a silver platter, keep the heat off him and his restaurant.

By the time Damon sauntered in, Jane had finished her research and was sitting at her desk munching a sandwich. She looked up with her mouth full and waved her sandwich at him.

He sat heavily beside her at his desk and unloaded his laptop. What work had he been doing at home?

She finished chewing and wiped her mouth. "Are you okay?"

"Are *you* okay? I heard about the accident." He clenched a hand on the back of his neck. "I was going to call you, but…"

He offered up no good reason why he hadn't called his partner after finding out she'd been in a crash.

"A bit sore, but thank goodness we jumped from the car before it went over."

"God, I blame myself." He pinched the bridge of his nose.

"Why would you say that?" Jane carefully folded over one corner of the yellow wax paper from her sandwich.

"What?" Damon jerked his head up. "I—I mean I should've gone to that restaurant with you to question Ivan Kozlov. That's what you think happened, right? You questioned him, got too close and he sent some goons after you?"

"I'm not sure. I do believe the attack on me and Agent Ruskin is related to the case, but I had left the restaurant hours before. I don't believe your presence at the interview would've prevented the truck coming after us or not...do you?"

"Wait, when did this happen? I thought you were followed and got hit after you left the interview with Ivan." Damon's red-rimmed eyes popped above the hand clamped over his mouth.

The guy looked exhausted...and on edge.

"I completed my uneventful interviews at the restaurant, and Ivan even sent me away with some borscht. I went home, had my soup and went out again with Agent Ruskin. It happened at that point."

Jane took another bite of her sandwich, watching Damon contort his face from the corner of her eye. He was dying to ask her where she and Tim went. Hadn't he read her report? She'd mentioned interviewing a witness, but hadn't released his name. She wanted to protect Max as much as possible—even if that meant protecting him against a cop.

Damon logged on to his laptop and rolled his shoulders. "I'm sorry I wasn't there."

"Did you get things straightened out with the kids last night?" She crumpled her sandwich wrapper and stuffed it in the bag. "I thought you were picking them up today from school."

"Yeah, I still am. The ex and I just had to clear up some other issues." He scooted his chair close to hers and dropped his voice. "I'm really sorry about all this drama, but I know you understand."

"I do, Damon. Take care of the kids." She tossed her bag into the trash can.

She did have drama with her divorce, but she'd never taken it to work. But Damon had more than divorce drama going on in his life, and she had the unpleasant task of exposing it. Even if he weren't working with Ivan on the sly, he had a duty to reveal his ties to Sissy and the restaurant.

The fact that he'd concealed this from her gave her a queasy stomach.

Her phone buzzed with a text, and she read that Tim couldn't get next to Sissy today but had plans for tonight. He wanted her to call to discuss.

Clearing her throat, she stood up. "Ladies' room, if anyone cares."

She pocketed her phone and made a beeline for her car in the parking lot.

She dropped onto the seat of her work car, which she'd be using for a few days until she got a rental delivered. She tapped Tim's name on her phone, and he picked up after the first ring.

Without even saying hello, he jumped in with, "How are you feeling?"

"Sore, stiff and bruised. How about you?"

"Same, but I meant from the accident."

A silly grin claimed her face. "If you were next to me, I'd punch you for that."

"If you were next to me, I'd kiss you—and all your sore, stiff and bruised spots." He huffed out a breath. "Seriously, no lingering ailments? You don't need to go to the hospital? See a doctor?"

"I'm fine. Hell, I've survived an explosion and a truck ramming. Bring it on now, baby." She waved at her lieutenant as he walked past her car.

"And you survived sex in the front seat of a Mercedes."

The heat rushed to her face, as if she were a teenager who'd just lost her virginity instead of a grownup, divorced woman and cop. She whispered, "I barely survived that."

"We need a repeat performance, without the bangup ending."

"Did you call me to discuss our sex life? Because I have something to share with you." She glanced in her rearview mirror at her shining eyes and soft lips. This conversation had just shaved ten years off her life.

"Me first." He took a sip of something. "I made contact with Sissy, at her gym, of all places."

"You hit on her in the gym?" Something akin to

jealousy sliced the back of her neck, or maybe that was the ibuprofen wearing off.

"I got her address and followed her, and that's the first place she went. I happened to have a gym bag in my car with some sweaty workout clothes, so I joined her, pumping iron. Made a few moves, got her number and she agreed to meet up tonight."

"Not very loyal to Damon, is she?"

"I think Damon might serve a very specific purpose for her. She may have roped him in for Ivan."

"Speaking of Damon, he was late today, and I noticed he'd put away the picture of him and the woman I thought was his girlfriend."

"You know for a fact she isn't? Maybe Damon isn't very loyal to Sissy, either." Tim cleared his throat.

"One of the other detectives told me that picture was of Damon and his sister."

"Did Damon tell you that was his woman?"

She squeezed her eyes shut. "I don't remember. I could've just assumed. Anyway, he came in today, blaming himself for our accident."

He sucked in a sharp breath. "Really? Just like that?"

"Not just like that. He meant it in a vague way that he should've been at Ivan's with me—or at least that's what he said. The man looked wrecked."

"Maybe because he just set up his partner, and she survived."

"I don't know, but I feel sick to my stomach over it." She sniffled. "Where and when are you meeting Sissy? Not at Ivan's?"

"When she gets off work. You don't think I need to worry about a jealous Damon showing up, do you?"

"Not tonight. He's with his kids. Maybe when the cat's away, Sissy will play. Where are you meeting her?"

"The Purple Orchid. It's a tiki bar on Hollywood Boulevard. She's waitressing at Ivan's, so she's off at ten." He snorted. "I'll be sure to wear a Hawaiian shirt."

"I know that bar. That's a sketchy area of Hollywood."

"All areas of Hollywood are sketchy these days."

"Okay, a *particularly* sketchy area. Watch your back."

"Yes, ma'am. I wanted to let you know, anyway. I'll insinuate myself with her and report back."

"Don't insinuate yourself with her the same way you insinuated yourself with me."

"This is work. That wasn't." He paused for a few seconds, waiting for her normal objection but she didn't have one this time. Then he said, "You watch your back, too."

"I'm having dinner with a friend tonight, but I'll be waiting up for your update."

They ended the call, and Jane slipped back into the station where Damon was still reviewing video from the San Pedro docks.

"No luck on that, yet?" She jabbed a finger at his monitor.

"Nothing." He stretched. "I got another hour before picking up the kids. Anything you want me working on?"

Yeah, the truth.

"Keep doing what you're doing. I have to make a few personal calls to get my insurance and rental car straightened out."

Damon whistled. "That was a nice car. That's gotta hurt."

She flicked her fingers. "My ex bought it. Probably a good thing it's gone."

"It's good to have money like that." He shook his head.

Jane bit her lip as she scrolled for the number of her insurance company. Damon had been making comments about her financial situation ever since they were partnered. Was this all about money to him? He had a rude awakening coming his way.

TIM STEPPED INTO The Purple Orchid and squinted into the darkness. The neon palm trees cast a pink and green glow over the bar, and the crack of pool cue against ball resounded from the back room. He hoped Sissy didn't want a game of pool, but if that loosened her tongue, he'd sharpen his cue.

She had to know Damon was a cop. Had to know whether or not he had private meetings with Ivan. Did she also know what happened to Lana? He counted on his fingers. Time was running out for Lana.

As his eyes adjusted to the gloom, he spotted Sissy on a barstool, wiggling her fingers in the air at him.

He made his way toward her, the pink neon giving her a halo. He hoped she earned that tonight. She could be an angel to a lot of people, but he'd have to go slow. He claimed the stool next to her and took her hand. "You're here."

She smiled and glanced at him through her lowered lashes. "You think I stand you up?"

Jane never played flirtatious games like this. She didn't have to.

"You never know." He lifted his shoulders, his leather jacket creaking. "I've had a few dating mishaps. You?"

"Mishaps?" She tilted her head, and a swath of blond hair fell over her bare shoulder.

"Like mistakes." He could speak to her in her native tongue, but that would put her on alert. He'd play her game.

"Yes, many mishap." She shoved a brightly colored concoction at him, a skewer of fruit balanced across the top. "From me."

He pinched the short stem of the glass and held up the drink. "Not necessary."

"It's house special." She wrinkled her pert nose. "Very weak, but you like and then we drink beer."

"Or vodka?" He took a sip of the sweet drink and almost gagged. "Don't you Russians drink vodka?"

"Only good stuff." She flicked her mane of hair over her shoulder and had several men at the bar craning their necks to see what she'd do next. Tim could almost excuse Damon and his fascination with her. "I drink beer in America…and sometimes fruity drinks."

She clinked her glass with his and took a dainty sip, while he sucked up half of his.

He massaged his temple against the brain freeze. "Not strong, but cold."

She waved her hand with its long, sculptured finger-nails. "I still waiting for warm LA weather."

"How long have you been here?" He bit into the pineapple, and some juice ran down his chin. Good thing he didn't care if he impressed Sissy or not.

She put a jewel-studded fingernail to her lips and raised her eyes. "November."

Lana had arrived in the US after that. Sissy must've known her at the restaurant.

"Make a lot of friends here?" He slurped up the dregs of his drink and pushed it away, almost knock-ing the glass over. He shook his head.

Sissy's hand shot out and grabbed the glass. "Whoa. I paying for drink not glass."

He rubbed his eyes. "Too much sugar. Friends?"

"I make friends easy." She pointed at her deep cleav-age. "You be my friend?"

"Yeah, sure." He had to get beyond the weather and drinks with her.

Leaning forward, she squeezed his thigh, close to his crotch. "I show you friendly."

"I…" He licked his lips, so dry after finishing that sweet drink.

She whispered in his ear. "We go outside for friendly time."

Friendly time? His muscles, aching from the acci-dent all day, felt loose and pliable now.

Sissy took his arm and pulled him up. "We go out-side."

He wanted to sit down. He didn't want to be friendly

with anyone but Jane. He opened his mouth to protest, but his thick tongue wouldn't move the way he wanted it to move.

His legs wobbled as he stood up, moving only when Sissy propelled him forward. He tried to dig his heels into the floor to stop his forward progress, but nothing seemed to work.

Her long fingernails dug into the leather of his jacket, and he felt the pressure on his arm.

She huddled close to him, her body pressed against his, but instead of affection, menace radiated from her in waves.

He tried to jerk his arm from hers, but his muscle responded to his brain with a twitch. She squeezed harder and breathed into his ear.

"We going to back for talk. That what you want, *FBI man*?"

His eyes drifted shut, and then flew open when Sissy pushed through the heavy metal door, pushing him outside in front of her. The slap of cool air on his face pricked his senses, and he took a deep breath to clear his senses. The smell of garbage invaded his nostrils instead and he gagged.

Sissy grabbed him and shoved him against the wall of the building. He felt like a limp pile of spaghetti in her hands.

She got in his face and hissed. "Stay out of our business."

Spittle landed on his cheeks, and his head flopped to the side.

She slammed him against the wall again before releasing her hold, and he began to sink to the ground. As his eyelids fluttered and his heartbeat pounded in his ears, he heard footsteps to his left.

Sissy growled. "I got him out here. Now take care of him."

Chapter Nineteen

Jane sidled into the dark bar and flicked a lock from her blond wig back from her face. Tim wasn't the only one who had undercover skills.

She scanned The Purple Orchid as she sauntered inside, her hands itching to tug at her short skirt. The bar wasn't as crowded as she thought it would be, and her entrance drew plenty of unwanted attention—but no Tim and no Sissy.

Her nostrils flared, and the apprehension she'd been feeling all night barreled into her chest. She eased onto a barstool and didn't even have to signal the bartender.

He stationed himself in front of her, flicking a white bar towel over his shoulder. "What can I get you?"

"White wine, please."

"You're at The Purple Orchid. Are you sure you don't want one of our specialty drinks? They look pretty, but they can kick your ass."

"My ass is fine. I'm good with wine." She swiveled the stool side to side, looking for Tim. Instead, she got a beefy guy with a long beard and tattooed neck in her line of sight.

Hoisting his girth onto a stool, he put his beer bottle down almost in front of her. "Two hot blondes in one night, and I'm hoping to get lucky with number two."

Jane's pulse quickened. "What happened to the other blonde?"

"She was already hooked up." He smacked a wide hand on the bar. "Her drink's on me, Frankie."

"You mean she walked in here alone, snagged someone and walked out again?" Jane straightened out the cocktail napkin Frankie had tossed her way.

"That's what happened, sugar." He winked. "Maybe you and me can do the same."

Jane's lips tightened. Tim had left with Sissy? How could he be so stupid?

Frankie placed her wine on the napkin. "I doubt this lady's gonna be dumb enough to follow you out back, Derek."

"Out back?" Jane's fingers curled around the stem of her wineglass.

"That's where they went." Frankie jerked his thumb over his shoulder. "The guy downed one of our purple passions and she led him right out back. Told ya they were kick-ass."

Jane hopped from the stool, knocking over her glass of wine and stepping on Derek's big foot in the process. With his yelp behind her, she dashed toward the back of the room and drove her hip against the metal door as she smacked her hands on the silver release bar.

She staggered into the alley and almost tripped over Sissy, who squeaked. Beyond Sissy's head, she saw a man half dragging Tim toward a side street.

Sissy made a run for it, but Jane had more important business. She pulled her gun from her purse and in one fluid movement had it aimed at the man holding Tim. As she crept toward them, she yelled. "LAPD! Stop!"

The man who had a hold of Tim stumbled and glanced over his shoulder. If he had a gun on Tim, there wasn't anything she could do to save him.

She kicked off her high heels and charged toward them, bits of gravel, dirt and glass grinding into her bare feet. "Stop, or I'll shoot you."

A car drove up perpendicular to the alley, a few feet in front of Tim. She had to stop them now, or they'd take Tim. She couldn't allow that to happen—ever.

She squeezed off a shot to the left of Tim and his abductor, just to show she meant business. She shouted. "You're next."

Two seconds later, space appeared between Tim and the other man. Tim hit the ground, so Jane took another shot—this time aiming at the man's center mass.

A grunt echoed down the alley, and Tim's attacker threw himself at the waiting car.

Jane descended on him, her gun raised. Before she could take another shot, the man clambered into the car, which took off with a squeal.

She covered the remaining distance like a sprinter, and she fell to the ground next to Tim. "Are you all right? Did Sissy drug you?"

His head lolled to the side, and his mouth gaped open. She put her ear close to his lips, but all she got was his hot breath on her cheek—she'd take it.

She cradled his head in her lap and said, "It's okay, my love. You're going to be all right."

Two HOURS LATER, Jane sat by Tim's bedside at Cedars-Sinai Hospital, holding his hand. When he squeezed her fingers, her head shot up.

"You're awake."

"Awake but groggy as hell." He rubbed his mouth, and she hunched forward to get his water bottle and hold the plastic straw to his lips.

"Now you have an appreciation of what roofied women go through."

He sucked down half the bottle. "Am I drooling?"

"No." She dabbed the pad of her thumb against a drop of water on his chin. "Can you walk me through what happened, or don't you remember?"

"I met Sissy at the bar." He raised an eyebrow. "Where is the lovely Sissy?"

"Gone—for now. Go on."

"She was already there and had already ordered two drinks, some God-awful, sweet thing. Even without the drugs, I shouldn't have taken one sip. It was horrible, but I thought I could get into her good graces, get her guard down."

"It's you who had your guard down." She touched a finger to his nose, and he captured it with his hand. "So, she already knew who you were and drugged you."

"I don't think we can blame Damon for this one. He didn't know I was meeting Sissy, did he?"

"Of course not, but maybe Sissy is more loyal than we thought. Once you came onto her in the gym, maybe she reported that to Damon…or Ivan. Maybe Damon had already warned her about strange men trying to make her acquaintance."

"You've seen Sissy. That must happen to her a lot. I doubt she reports every encounter to Damon."

"Maybe not typically, but my partner must be on high alert now. That's why he removed the picture of him and his sister from his desk at the station. He was nearly apoplectic when he found out I'd been out later, after my interview with Ivan. He was afraid I'd seen him at Ivan's—he was careless to go there that night."

Tim fake-smacked his face. "God, I'm so stupid. I must've thought I was irresistible or something to have Sissy so readily agree to meet me."

She pulled his hand to her lips and pressed a kiss on his knuckles. "You are to me."

"And then to take that drink from her. My mind must've been elsewhere." His dark eyes burned into hers. "You saved my life again, Jane."

"Let's not start keeping score." Her cheeks burned. She'd rushed in there like a fool. She didn't even know if Tim's abductor had a gun. He could've killed Tim the minute she shot at him. Talk about having your mind elsewhere.

She took a deep breath, trying to go back to cop mode. "Sissy drugged you, lured you out to the alley and then turned you over to her accomplice?"

"That's about all I remember." He scratched his head. "The guy got away?"

"Yeah, he literally had a getaway car waiting for him. I think he was planning to take you away." She shivered. "Maybe they didn't want to leave a dead FBI agent in an alley in Hollywood. Maybe Ivan wanted to question you."

"Whatever their plans, you saved me from them." He trailed his nails along her inner arm to her wrist.

She shivered some more.

"I think you had a hand in that. You must've gathered up some strength from somewhere and pushed off from him. Once I saw that separation, I took my shot."

"You nailed him?"

She nodded. "Don't worry. You were on the ground at that point. I had a clear shot."

"I would never doubt your judgment."

Tim still wasn't thinking clearly if he thought that was a good move on her part. She held up one finger. "We do have his blood, so any DNA we can get from Ivan's employees should give us a match."

"Car?"

"Dark blue compact, a beater with no plates."

"Suspect?"

She sighed. "White guy, about your height, stocky build, black stocking cap—and bleeding."

"I'm in for some ribbing at the Bureau. Taken in by a woman, and then saved by a woman."

"I thought that stuff didn't bother you." She cocked her head. "Better than dying."

"Any day. Besides, you're not just any woman."

"Right answer." She smoothed the sheets on either side of his body. She'd have to question Damon now, or somebody would. Maybe it would be better if she left it to someone else.

"What's wrong?" Tim pinched her chin.

"I'm thinking about my partner."

"Bad break. It's always hard when it's one of our own."

"Do you think I should turn that job over to someone else?" Jane folded his sheet into pleats with nervous fingers.

"No. You need to question him yourself, Jane. It's your case. He's your partner." He patted her hand. "I can be with you, if you want. I'm part of the case, too. I'm the one his girlfriend tried to whack."

"You're right." She covered her eyes with her hand. "I hope he wasn't involved in trying to get you abducted... or killed."

Tim's jaw tightened. "He'd better hope he wasn't. I'm pretty sure he was responsible for the explosion at Austin's container. If not responsible, he tipped them off."

"If you're going in hard like that, it's better I question him by myself." She wagged a finger at him. "I'm going to extend him certain courtesies, but this has to be done by the book."

"By the book." He thumped his chest with his fist. "That's me."

The nurse bustled into the room, sparing Tim her response. "I see you're awake. Are you feeling better, Tim? We gave you an IV to flush some of the toxins from your body. You should be feeling better than ever."

"I feel fine. I'm out this morning, right?"

"Yes, the doctor's going to check in with you before you leave, and then you're on your way." She leveled a finger at Jane. "Is this your ride?"

Tim grinned. "She's my ride, my savior, my everything."

The nurse tipped her head at Jane. "Aren't you the lucky one?"

"I think he's still feeling the effects of the drugs." Jane rolled her eyes, but a warm glow surrounded her heart.

The nurse plopped a plastic bag containing Tim's clothes from last night at the foot of the bed. "You can get dressed before the doctor comes in."

When the nurse left, Jane squeezed Tim's foot beneath the sheet while she eyed the dirty clothes. "I should've brought you fresh duds. I'll let you get ready. I'm going to set up this meeting with Damon."

Jane made her way to the hospital's lobby and strolled outside into the sunshine. She leaned against the outside of the building, waiting for the spring warmth to seep into her body. She'd almost lost Tim last night, and she was about to lose a partner today.

She scrolled through her contacts and called Damon's cell. He picked up after the first ring.

"Jane."

"Damon, we need to talk."

He paused. "How's Tim? I—I heard you two had another...situation last night."

"C'mon, Damon. You know damn well the *situation*, if you wanna call a drugging and attempted abduction that, initiated with your girlfriend, Sissy."

The silence stretched between them. Had he hung up on her? "Damon?"

"I didn't know, Jane."

She released a slow breath from her nostrils. At least he wasn't going to deny the basics. "Like I said, we need to talk. You need to tell me what you do know. These are young women at risk, Damon. Think of your daughter."

He uttered something between a sob and a grunt and then whispered. "Not here, Jane. Not at the station. You owe me that."

She wasn't sure she owed a corrupt cop much of anything, even if he was her partner.

His voice hardened at her pause. "You really want to do it here where everyone can see Jane Falco destroy another partnership?"

She gritted her teeth. Was that why he'd asked to partner with her? Did he figure she'd let his garbage slide because she already had a rep of chewing through partners?

"I didn't destroy this partnership, Damon, but I'll give you a break if you promise to tell me everything."

He let out a noisy breath. "I do. I'm done with this, Jane. I only did it to protect Sissy."

And to make money and get a career boost. "Let's meet outside at Tommy's Burgers in North Hollywood. Noon."

"I can do that. Are you coming to the station today? We can drive over together."

"Not doing that." She rubbed two fingers across her forehead. "I have to get my friend out of the hospital."

She hung up on his apology.

By the time she returned to Tim's room, the doctor had come and gone and Tim had gotten dressed. He was head to toe in black, in a form-fitting T-shirt, black jeans and motorcycle boots. "No wonder Sissy wanted to take you out back," she said, eyeing him.

"Yeah, right—to get me killed. You know that game? Kill, marry, f—"

She cut him off with a hand slicing through the air. "I get the point. Let's go. We have a meeting with Damon at twelve, if you're still in."

"Just like that?" He tossed his jacket over his shoulder. "You're not doing this at the station?"

"I'm extending him some professional courtesy. If he's crooked, the rest of the department will find out soon enough. I'm giving him a chance to explain himself to me first."

"How do you know he's not walking you into an ambush, Jane?"

"Call it gut instinct, just like the instinct that told me your meeting with Sissy was fraught with danger."

"Okay, I trust that instinct. Can you take me back to The Purple Orchid so I can get my car? Then I need to go home and change."

"I can do all that. The department is doing an investigation because I discharged my weapon off duty."

He widened his eyes. "They're not suspending you, are they? Because I can set them straight. You saved my life."

"No suspension. I told my lieutenant I'm close to solving the Russian Doll murders. With Max's statement and an investigation into Natalya's fledgling call-girl business, I think we can make a firm link between Ivan and Natalya's death."

"We still need to nail Ivan. As far as anyone else

knows, he's a kindly restaurateur providing jobs to the community and dispensing borscht."

"Maybe we'll get that proof at lunch today. If Damon turns witness, he can save himself a lot of trouble. It won't save his job, but it just might keep him out of prison."

"Then let's get that out of Damon. Maybe he can tell us what happened to Lana, and help us shut down the next shipment of women."

"And that's worth keeping Damon out of prison."

As THE SUN hit its peak in the sky, Jane parked her work sedan in a public lot, flashing her badge to the parking attendant.

He waved her to a spot on the edge of the lot.

Tim whistled. "So that's how the LAPD always gets the prime spots."

"We have to, if we ever hope to get any business done in this city." She snatched her jacket from the back seat. "Don't tell me you Fibbies never throw your weight around for perks."

"Shh." He held his finger to his lips. "Listen, you talk to Damon. Get the goods out of him, and I'll watch the perimeter for incoming threats."

"And if one of Damon's criminal associates takes me out, you know what to do."

Tim leaned over the console suddenly and cupped her face with his hand. "Don't even joke about that, Jane. Now that I have you back in my life, I'm never letting you go."

She turned and kissed his palm. "Who said I was joking?"

They both exited the vehicle and hiked up the block to Tommy's hamburger stand. Damon hadn't arrived yet.

She squinted, cupping her hand over her eyes. "I hope he didn't decide to do a runner. He'll never see his kids again if he tries that."

"And we'll be out a prime witness." Tim claimed a round table with benches attached and a blue-and-white-striped umbrella flapping above it. "This is a good spot, right in the middle."

He checked under the table, and then proceeded to look beneath every table on the patio. He strode to the counter and chatted with the employee for several minutes before walking away with three sodas.

She raised her eyebrows at him when he set down two of the drinks on the table.

"He said nobody suspicious has been hanging around, and he's been here since opening time at ten thirty."

"People actually eat Tommy's burgers at ten thirty in the morning?" She clamped a hand to her stomach in mock horror, but it was really to calm the butterflies assaulting her innards.

"Here's the man of the hour." Tim tipped his chin toward the sidewalk.

Damon, hunched forward with his hands in his pockets, lumbered up the street, his head down, the sun gleaming on his bald head.

"He looks defeated already." Jane held her breath, watching his progress.

"That's good. You don't have to break him down. Just let him talk. Are you recording him?"

"Damn straight." She plopped her phone on the table.

Damon lifted his head as he neared the table and his gaze darted to Tim. "What's he doing here?"

"Riding shotgun. It's his case, too, remember?" She brushed the hair from her face and straightened her shoulders. She did not cause this problem. "You *should* remember. Your girlfriend set him up last night."

"I wasn't involved in that." He shoved his hands in front of him, warding off the accusation. "I had no idea Sissy was meeting him. She didn't tell me, but if you don't think Ivan has warned off all his people against cops and Feds, you don't know how he works."

"That's what I'm here for—to find out how he works. To find out when he decided to murder Natalya for encroaching on his territory and how he found out Austin had been collecting tokens from the women he was trafficking."

Damon swallowed. "You know a lot. You know more than you've been telling me."

"Good thing, too." She tapped her phone in the middle of the table. "I'm going to record this, and I'm going to read you your rights, Damon."

"You're arresting me?" He half rose from his seat, and Tim laid a heavy hand on Damon's shoulder.

"Just an interrogation now. You have to face the music eventually, Damon. You know I can't promise you anything, but the more you give us, the more it'll help you out. You know the game."

Tim released his hold on her former partner and strolled to the other edge of the patio, his eyes on the patrons filling up the tables for lunch.

Damon ran a hand over the beads of sweat that had formed on his head and took a long drink of his soda. "I understand. If you don't get this guy, I'll need witness protection."

"Okay, let's get started." Jane tapped the red button on her phone to start recording.

"Damon Carter, you have the right—"

"Jane, get down!" Tim's voice roared across the patio.

She didn't even think twice. She dove under the table amid a hail of bullets and ear-splitting screams from the table next to her.

A slight pause and then two more shots. A squeal of tires. Somebody sobbed and a baby wailed. Then Damon slumped to the ground, blood pouring from a gaping wound in his head.

Inches away from her face, she watched the life drain from her former partner as he gurgled his dying words through a spurt of blood.

Chapter Twenty

As the dark blue sedan zigzagged into traffic, Tim flew to the table where Jane and Damon had been sitting a few seconds before the gunfire erupted. He dove beneath it, and choked out a breath at the trickle of blood meandering into the strands of Jane's hair splayed on the cement patio.

"Jane." He grabbed her arm, and she rolled her head toward him, her face pale, blood trickling from the bandage over her eyebrow.

"Is it over?"

He closed his eyes as relief swept through his body, making him weak. "A-are you okay? Are you hit?"

"I'm all right." She brought her knees to her chest and flung out an arm toward Damon's body, curled up next to her. "Damon's been shot. I think he's dead."

Sirens cascaded around them. Tim didn't even have to call 911. Plenty of witnesses already had their phones out, some recording the scene. He didn't know if the spray of bullets from the sedan had caught any bystanders in its arc. His every thought had been for Jane.

"Come on." Tim helped Jane from beneath the table

and led her away from Damon. When he had her seated at another table, he returned and checked Damon's pulse. Its stillness didn't surprise him, given the condition of the detective's head.

Straightening up, he scanned the crowd but didn't see any other injured parties, at least from gunshots. The gunman from the car had only one table in the sights of his AK-47. Tim waved his arm at one of the first uniforms on the scene.

The female cop had her gun drawn when she strode toward him. "What happened here? Where did the gunfire originate?"

Pointing to the street, Tim said, "It came from a dark blue sedan, maybe a Crown Vic. I didn't get the license plate, and the gunman had a mask on. I returned fire. Two shots. I may have hit the door."

As the officer raised her eyebrows, Tim whipped out his badge. "My LAPD counterpart, Detective Jane Falco, and I had a meeting with another LAPD detective regarding a case. He's dead."

"Were they the target of this ambush?" She was already snapping her fingers at another uniform, waving him over.

"I believe they were, yes. Definitely Detective Carter, maybe Detective Falco." Ivan and his Bratva buddies wanted to make sure Damon kept his mouth shut about what he knew. Had Jane gotten anything out of him before he died?

He didn't get a chance to ask Jane for the next hour as the police swarmed the scene, taking statements from the witnesses—none of whom were seriously hurt—collecting spent cartridges from the street and examining Damon's body.

He peered at Jane, head together with her lieutenant, who'd materialized on the scene as soon as word got out that one of their own had been hit. The lieutenant had been keeping Jane isolated on the patio, shielding her from too many questions. Had she told him yet what she and her partner had been about to discuss?

As if sensing his scrutiny, the lieutenant glanced Tim's way and gestured him over. Tim let out a long breath and squared his shoulders for the encounter. If this guy had any intention of laying the blame for this shooting on Jane, he'd set him straight.

Tim nodded when he joined them and sidled up next to Jane. Her wide, glassy eyes and disheveled hair made him want to put his arm around her, but she wouldn't appreciate that any more than her lieutenant would.

Jane cleared her throat and shoved an errant strand of hair, sticky with Damon's blood, behind her ear. "Lieutenant Figueroa, this is FBI Special Agent Ruskin."

The lieutenant thrust out his hand first, saying, "Agent, call me Fig. Everyone does."

Tim blinked. Not as adversarial as he'd anticipated. "You can call me Tim. Did Jane fill you in on our meeting with Detective Carter?"

"She did." Fig scratched his chin. "An unfortunate circumstance. I was just telling Jane, Internal Affairs was about to open a case on Detective Carter due to his financial difficulties. Can't say this is a surprise, but I'm sorry it went down like this. You saw the shooter. Russian mob?"

"He wasn't wearing a sign, but I'm sure Jane has informed you that they've been dogging us every step of this investigation."

"I have been telling him." Jane rubbed her pink-stained hands together in an obvious attempt to rid herself of Damon's blood. "I also told him we've narrowed the focus of our investigation to Ivan Kozlov. We have Max, we have Sissy and we have Damon. That's enough to get us a search warrant for Ivan's and to interrogate the man himself."

"Did you get anything out of Damon before…?"

Her gaze darted to Fig's face. "We had just started the interview. I was reading him his rights when the gunfire erupted."

"Damn." Tim slammed his fist into his palm. "So, nothing."

Fig folded his arms over his chest. "I wouldn't say nothing."

Jane said, "Before he died, as he was bleeding out next to me, he had a few words left to say—'rescue the girls before it's too late.'"

LATER THAT EVENING at Jane's house, Tim finally got to hold her in his arms. They sat close together on her couch with the drapes drawn. He stroked her hair, clean and shiny, with no trace of Damon's blood.

"How'd it go back at the station?"

"Everyone was in shock, but nobody knows why he was a target." She laced her fingers together in her lap. "Fig and I are keeping it hush-hush for now. We don't want to tip off Bratva or Ivan while we're getting the search warrant for the restaurant together."

He placed one hand over hers. "Is that hard for you? Are they looking at you, wondering why he got shot and you didn't?"

"Something like that. I can take it. They'll find out soon enough when we serve the warrant and bring in Ivan." She disentangled her fingers from his and rubbed her eye. "What I can't take is Damon's kids. He has two young children. Why would he jeopardize all that?"

"People do stupid things for money. Has IA confirmed that he's been getting payoffs?"

"They found bundles of cash in his home. It looks suspicious."

"While they investigate Damon, we're still looking at all the rest—Natalya's murder, Austin's. Ivan didn't murder those two to cover for a dirty cop. We know he wanted to shut down Natalya's competing operation, and Austin had information about the trafficking. That's why he had that storage unit at the docks in San Pedro. And what about Damon's last words?"

"It sounds like something is imminent, doesn't it?" She trapped her hands between her bouncing knees. "Earlier I reminded Damon that he had a daughter. That must've gotten to him. Those mementos Austin had in the unit must belong to women Ivan has captured. If we're to believe Damon, Ivan still has those women in his clutches. I wonder what he's waiting for?"

"Hang on." Tim scooted forward, reaching for his

phone. "It was just about a month ago when we raided the warehouse in San Pedro and came up short. The traffickers had already moved the women. We did some research into Russian merchant ships in port around that time and came up with a few possibilities."

He scrolled through his phone to locate the file with the list of ships docked at San Pedro that night. He read the names of the ships aloud. "The *Admiral Ushkov*, *MV Akademik Karpinsky* and the *SS Smolensk*. All were in port that week. We figured any one of those ships could've taken aboard the human cargo."

"What about this week?" Jane tugged on his sleeve. "Can you get that information for this week? It could give us a lead."

"I need your laptop. I have to log in with my CAC to get into this database. The Coast Guard approved our access to the data last time, and the card's good for a year."

Jane scrambled from the couch, her eyes lighting up for the first time since the shooting this afternoon. She pounced on her laptop case and dragged out her computer. "This should work. I have a card reader on it."

She settled the laptop in front of him on the coffee table and plugged it in. When it powered on, Tim shoved his Common Access Card in the slot on the side of the computer and connected to the FBI network. He delved into the shipping database.

Jane hovered over his arm, pressing her shoulder against his. "That's San Pedro, right?"

"Yeah, nothing leaving this week. A ship departed two days ago, but we'd be too late to rescue the women."

He squinted at the screen. "The next one is leaving in a week. That could be it, but I have a problem with San Pedro. Bratva knows we're all over the docks there. Would they be that daring to risk another departure from San Pedro?"

Their eyes met and at the exact same time, they both said, "Long Beach."

"That would make sense. Even though the port at San Pedro is busier, Long Beach might offer them more control—especially with us crawling all over the docks." He tapped the keyboard to switch to the different port and entered the same search criteria. "Hello."

"The *SS Dimitry Laptev.*" Jane jabbed her finger at the ship's name on the screen. "It leaves tonight at midnight. Pacific Route, making stops in Taiwan and Malaysia. This could be it, Tim."

"Not so fast." He nudged her finger aside with his own. "There are two more this week—the *MV Mekhanik Tarasov* and the *Kapitan Man*. It could be any one of them."

"But this one is tonight. We can start with this one."

He slouched back against the couch and massaged his temples. "Maybe we could, but we're a long way from getting a search warrant for that ship or any Russian cargo ship. Can you imagine the international dustup if we boarded the *Dimitry Laptev* and found—cargo?"

"Okay." She jumped from the couch and paced to the kitchen. "It would be easier to get a warrant for the containers and warehouses at the Port of Long Beach than the ship itself. We could begin our search there. If we find the women, we may not have to board that vessel."

Tim folded his hands behind his head and tipped back to stare at the ceiling. "I don't know about the LAPD, Jane, but the FBI is gonna have a hard time getting a judge to sign off on a warrant in the middle of the night based on the dying words of a crooked cop. Your department doesn't even have the warrant for Ivan's restaurant, yet."

"You're right, but there could be women in danger right now." She wrung her hands in front of her. "I can't...you know I have a hard time with that."

He pushed up from the couch and wrapped her in a hug. "I know."

The doorbell startled them, breaking them apart. Tim went immediately to his weapon on the kitchen table and held a finger to his lips.

His heart slammed against his chest as Jane crept to the side of the large double door. She tilted her head to peer through the peephole and put a hand to the slim column of her throat.

Backing away from the door, she whispered to Tim. "It's a woman."

He hissed back. "That doesn't mean anything. Remember, there's a female sniper out there who has you in her sights."

Tim put out his arm to urge Jane away from the door and did his own reconnaissance. When he looked through the peephole, his mouth dropped open, and he fumbled for the dead bolt.

Jane materialized behind him in a second, grabbing his arm. "What are you doing? Who is it?"

He released the locks and threw open the door on the pretty brunette, whose lips curved into a shy smile.

As he pulled her inside, he said over his shoulder. "It's Lana."

Chapter Twenty-One

Jane clapped both hands over her heart. Had the women gotten away? Had someone freed them already? Had Ivan let them go after the debacle with Damon?

Her head swam and she braced a hand against the doorjamb to steady herself. "Are you all right, Lana?"

The young woman nodded and shoved her hands in the pockets of her hoodie. "I am okay."

"Lana, this is Jane. She's with the LAPD, and she's been working the murder cases of Natalya and Austin. Do you know about those murders?"

"I know." She rubbed her nose. "Natalya not bad, but so foolish. She think she do better business than Ivan. Nobody cross Ivan."

Jane eyed Lana's pale face. "Where have you been? How did you know to come here?"

"I just… I am thirsty. Maybe something to drink, please?" The young woman swayed on her feet, and Jane lunged forward to catch her at the same time Tim grabbed Lana's arm.

As Lana put her hand on her stomach, Jane wrapped

hers around her waist. "Sit down. I'll get you something. Questions can come later."

Lana turned to her with tears in her eyes. "Thank you, Jane. Alexei said you help."

Tim asked, "You've been in touch with your brother?"

"Save the questions, Tim. I'll…" Jane paused as she watched Lana drop her other hand to her midsection, cradling her belly.

"You're pregnant." Jane sealed her lips. That wasn't her news to blurt out. "I'm sorry. Sit down and I'll get you something to eat."

Lana waved her hand. "It's okay. Tim already know. But not Alexei?"

Lana had directed the question at Tim and he answered. "I haven't told him, but knowing about your pregnancy only increased my concern. I knew the Bratva traffickers wouldn't want a pregnant sex slave."

"I told you I wouldn't let no one take baby." She rubbed her belly. "Baby maybe save me. Maybe without baby I wouldn't face danger to protect."

Tim glanced at Jane. "Sometimes we take the greatest risks for others."

As Tim settled Lana on the couch, Jane grabbed a container of leftover pasta from the fridge. She stuck the pasta in the microwave and poured a glass of milk and one of water. When the microwave beeped, she carried the food and drink to the living room.

Lana had tucked one foot beneath her and reached for the pasta when Jane placed it on the coffee table. The young woman wolfed down half the contents of the container before stopping for a breath and some water.

Jane tapped the glass. "Drink that milk, too. Are you taking prenatal vitamins?"

Tim rolled his eyes and pointed to his watch.

"No, no doctor yet." Lana picked up the milk and downed it. She then finished the pasta, scraping the bottom of the plastic container with her fork.

"I'm going to get you more food, and Tim's going to ask you some questions." She took the empty container from Lana and shot Tim a pointed look.

He got right down to business. "Did Ivan let you go, or did you escape?"

"I escape. I knew what was happen. I knew Ivan pick me." She sniffed. "Natalya help me. When she find out I pregnant, she knew I wouldn't work for her—and I didn't want to. She hide me. Then she die."

Tim raised his eyebrows at Jane as she delivered a plate of cheese, crackers and fruit. He asked, "Did Ivan kill Natalya because she helped you, or because of her escort business?"

"Maybe both." Lana lifted her shoulders and then carefully balanced a piece of cheese on a cracker.

"Lana, did Natalya help the other women, too? The women that Ivan was going to take?" Jane handed Lana a napkin.

"No. He still has them." Lana clapped the napkin over her mouth as tears spilled over the rims of her eyes.

"Do you know where he's keeping them?" Tim hunched forward, his elbows on his knees, his brow furrowed.

"I don't know. Sorry I don't know." She dabbed her tears with the corner of the napkin. "When I saw Sissy's boyfriend on the TV, I knew was time to come out. Maybe safe now. I call my brother. He told me to come here. That Tim here and Tim's girlfriend Jane. He meet me here."

Patting Lana's shoulder, Tim said, "We'll protect you, Lana, but we want to help those other women, too. We want to put a stop to Ivan's activities. We want to arrest him for ordering Natalya's murder and Austin's."

"Me, too." She put a hand over her heart. "I lucky, but I don't want them hurt."

"Is there anything you can remember? You said you knew that you were a target for Ivan. You must've heard him, or someone else, talking about the plan to know that you were part of it." Jane scooped a hand through her hair in frustration. "Anything. A name? A place? A time?"

Lana tilted her head to the side. "Just one name I never hear before. Dimitry."

Jane's heart stuttered as she exchanged a look with Tim. "Dimitry? Dimitry who?"

"Dimitry..." Lana picked up a slice of apple, her nose wrinkling. "Lev... Laptev. Dimitry Laptev."

AN HOUR LATER, Jane was back in the kitchen telling Lana to help herself to anything in the fridge or cupboards. "You need to eat."

When the doorbell rang for the second time that night, Jane jumped. Alexei had texted Tim earlier and when he found out they were on their way to Long Beach, he wanted in. Tim told Alexei he had to get here before ten, and it looked like he'd just made it.

Tim checked the door, gun in hand, and then let Alexei inside. He immediately swept up his sister in a bear hug, towering above her.

Jane watched Lana tug her sweatshirt around her body as her face sported two red flags. She wasn't ready to tell her brother about her pregnancy, and her baby bump was small enough to hide. She could tell him when everyone was safe.

Jane slipped her backpack over one shoulder. She was about to go on a mission with Ukrainian special ops and a hardened FBI undercover agent. She'd be fine.

She took Lana by the shoulders. "Lock this door behind us, and don't open it for anyone—even the police. I am the police, and I'll be in Long Beach. Do you know how to use a gun?"

Alexei scoffed. "She's a Ukrainian woman from the village. She knows how to use a gun. She knows how to use Kalashnikov even."

"Well, I don't have a Kalashnikov, but I do have this pretty little .22." She retrieved the gun from a drawer and handed it to Lana. "Point, shoot and ask questions later."

"I can do that. Easy." She quirked one eyebrow. "But if dead, he don't ask questions later."

Jane held her fist out for a bump. "You'll do fine."

When they stepped outside with their gear, Jane listened for the dead bolt and then they loaded up Alexei's car. Neither she nor Tim had had any luck with their respective departments drafting search warrants for a wild-goose chase, as Captain Fields had called it.

It was a long drive from her place to Long Beach, but they'd get there with about an hour to spare before the ship was scheduled to depart. A lot could happen in that hour.

Alexei's car sailed off the 710 freeway toward the water. Tim directed him to the general area where the *Dimitry Laptev* was berthed, along with other welded-steel cargo ships sporting cranes and pallets.

Alexei parked the car in the corner, behind a cargo container, and the three of them slipped into the night. The salt air whipped across Jane's face, and she licked her lips.

They hunched forward, darting from building to building to conceal themselves from anyone watching. The clanging of metal and raised voices brought them up short, and Jane gazed out at the activity buzzing around the big gray ship, lit up like a Christmas tree.

She swallowed and whispered. "I didn't expect so many people. If they're all in the employ of Bratva and we try to stop this, we're in trouble."

Alexei answered gruffly. "They're not. Bratva buy cops, business, judges, maybe politicians back home, not shipping companies. These workers not protect them, and the dockworkers are American. Bratva have few contacts on ship to smooth things over, but nobody willing to die for them."

Tim poked Alexei in the back. "That's what we're looking for."

Jane glanced in the direction of his nod and saw safety vests, goggles and hard hats piled on a pallet, along with some tools. They'd fit right in.

Alexei jerked his thumb at Jane. "Should she go with us or act as lookout? I don't see many women on the docks."

Tim grunted. "Dude, she's as tall as most men. With the helmet, safety glasses and a loose-fitting vest, nobody's going to notice she's a woman."

"You take that from him?" Alexei punched Tim in the shoulder.

"I know what he means." Jane grinned. "And I'm not going to be the lookout."

Ten minutes later, outfitted like dockworkers, one by one they strode from their hiding place, as if they owned the place.

The workers were still delivering cargo containers to the berthing area of the ship, and cranes were positioned to hoist them onto the deck. Jane shivered at the thought of those young women huddled inside one of these containers, perhaps drugged, ill, frightened. They'd decided to fan out and try to get close to the containers to search each one.

As Jane walked toward the first container, she tried to widen her stance, lumber instead of sway, swing her arms. There had to be a few female dockworkers, so maybe her presence here wouldn't be surprising. She knew that most dockworkers also wore earplugs to block the noise at loading time, so there wouldn't be much conversation happening.

She sidled up next to the cold metal of the container and tapped on the outside with the screwdriver, which she'd grabbed from the pile of tools, clutched in her hand. Although shipping containers consisted of steel, all had doors and were not soundproof. Also, if Ivan hoped to keep these women alive for the journey, he'd have to include a container with air vents. If someone were trapped inside, surely, they'd hear her on the outside.

She continued down a line of containers waiting their turn for the cranes to pick them up and deposit them on the ship. She applied the same process to each—a few light taps on the outside, getting close to a gap in the container and whispering words of inquiry and encouragement. She pressed her ear to the gaps, listening for a response, a scrape, an answering whisper.

As she neared the end of the row, she paused, cocking her head. The hustle and bustle of the activity around the ship had faded a little, and the bright lights didn't extend this far. Jane rolled her shoulders and crept up to the next container. She went through her steps, placed her hands against the metal and whispered.

"Is anyone in there? I'm the police. I'm here to help you. Lana Savchenko sent me."

Closing her eyes, she held her breath and rested her forehead against the container. She smacked her palm against the metal and turned away.

That was when she heard it—a soft rustling sound beneath the clang of the metal. She spun around and pressed her eye to one of the open spaces in the container. "Hello? Is someone there?"

A breathless voice answered. "Help."

"We will. We are." Her heart skipped several beats.

"I'm going to get you out of there. We're going to get you out of there, all of you."

More noises emanated from the confined space—whimpers and gasps and sobs.

Jane held back her own sobs as she brushed her hands against the container, looking for the handles that would open it. She, Tim and Alexei hadn't even discussed this part. She shoved the screwdriver into the open gap, just to let the women know she hadn't abandoned them.

Glancing down, she spotted latches on the corner of the container. Those had to be a start. As she started to duck, a figure came around the corner and in one swift movement, a man had her by the throat, shoving her back against the container, the handle of the screwdriver gouging her spine.

"Jane, what's a nice girl like you doing out on the docks at night." Ivan appeared behind her attacker, holding a gun and clicking his tongue.

She gagged and clawed at the hand around her throat.

Ivan snapped his fingers, and the man released her, but not before snatching her weapon from its holster.

She coughed and rubbed her neck. "It's over, Ivan. We know you're behind the trafficking. You may have stopped Detective Carter from implicating you, but we have enough evidence against you. We have people willing to talk."

His jaw hardened, vanquishing the image of the avuncular restaurateur. "You know what happens to people who talk, Jane. Nobody will say one word against me, and at midnight the lovely ladies inside this container will be on their way to a new life."

She spit at his feet. "Over my dead body."

"As you like." He shrugged. "Where is your accomplice? The FBI agent? He thought he almost had me before, but Damon got wind of the operation and warned us. It's nice having people in the right places."

"I'm here alone, but I'm not letting you get away with this."

"I don't believe you." He chuckled and stepped closer to her, so close she could smell the food from the restaurant off his clothes. He held his gun to her head. "He's here somewhere, but Agent Ruskin won't be stupid enough to try anything. Or maybe he believes the lives of these Ukrainian whores are more important than your life."

"Do you hear that, Ruskin?" Ivan's head swiveled from side to side. "You come at me, Jane's dead."

While Ivan had his head turned, a brief shadow fell across the ground from above. Had Tim and Alexei managed to climb on top of the container? If Ivan stepped back and looked up, it would be all over.

Jane licked her lips. "Why did you have Natalya killed? Is it because she hid Lana or because of her escort service?"

He waved the gun slightly. If he did that again, she'd seize the opportunity.

"I don't care about Lana. Stupid girl got pregnant in the home country before she even got here. Useless to me." His eyes narrowed. "But Natalya didn't know her place. She could've helped me in my business—

recruiting women. She let her dreams get too big. She should've known her place. Just like you, Jane. You should've stayed married to your rich husband."

Jane tried to shift away from him, but his weapon tracked her. He was close enough that she might be able to make a grab for it, especially if Tim dropped from above and took care of the masked goon. Ivan's arms were crossed in front of him, her gun dangling from his fingertips.

"And Austin? Was he helping Natalya?"

"Austin wanted to make reparations for his father's crimes." Ivan huffed out a breath. "He told Natalya he'd help her recruit girls away from me, but he never would've allowed them to work for Natalya, either. He got too American—he wanted to be the cowboy with the white hat."

A pinging noise from above made all three of them jerk their heads back. Two bodies came hurtling off the top of the container, and a shot rang out. Tim flattened Ivan's accomplice, who managed to squeeze off another bullet to nowhere.

Alexei had missed his mark, glancing off Ivan's body, pushing him closer to Jane. Alexei rolled on the ground, writhing in pain, and Jane realized the first bullet had hit him.

Tim punched out the guy on the ground and squatted in a crouch, ready to lunge at Ivan. Alexei panted to the side, clutching his leg.

Ivan ground out between his teeth. "You two need to leave now, or I'm killing Jane."

Jane yelled. "You're not—"

With his free hand, Ivan punched her in the mouth.

Red rage thrummed through Jane's body. She'd vowed no man would ever hit her again. The handle of the screwdriver nudged her back again, and she shifted away from it.

When Ivan hit her, Tim had roared in anger and jumped up to his full height. The furious man in front of him caused Ivan to flinch and move even closer to Jane.

With her head pounding out a beat of revenge, Jane reached behind her back, yanked the screwdriver from the container and stabbed it into the side of Ivan's neck.

Epilogue

A week after she, Tim and Alexei had rescued the women from the shipping container, Jane parted the curtains to her deck and opened both doors. "Finish your coffee out here. It's a beautiful morning."

Alexei stepped onto the deck next to her, cradling his mug, one arm in a sling from the bullet wound in his shoulder. "No more snipers out there."

Tim took a seat and kicked his legs up on the railing. "I forgot to tell you, Jane. The DNA on the cigarette came back, and it matched Azra Balik's."

Despite the warmth of the sun, Jane curled her hands around her cup of steaming, hot coffee, her gaze darting toward the canyon. "She's still out there."

"Berlin." Tim brushed his hands together. "She was last traced to Germany. Ivan hired her for a quick job. I don't think he ever meant to kill you…at least not at first. He just wanted to terrorize you."

"Mission accomplished." She waved her arm over the canyon. "I'm glad I can enjoy my view again."

Lana came outside carrying another plate of food. "I took second helping."

"You don't watch out, that baby going to come out as big as his daddy, Arkidy." Alexei poked Lana's protruding belly.

"Hey, no touch." She slapped at her brother's hand.

He grinned. "Finish stuffing your face. We go back to your place to pack the rest of your things."

"Max will be there to help."

Jane wedged a hand on her hip, tilting her head at Lana. "Were you leading that poor boy on? He's half in love with you."

Tim grunted. "It's a good thing he is, or he probably wouldn't have helped us."

Lana stabbed several clumps of scrambled eggs with her fork and shoved the food into her mouth. Around the chews, she said, "He just nice guy."

Alexei stood up and stretched. He stuck out his hand to Tim. "Good working with you again, my brother."

Tim took his hand and squeezed Alexei's shoulder. "Will always have your back."

Alexei turned to Jane and swept her into a hug. "Now you have a good woman to have your back when I'm not here."

Lana dropped her plate and made it a group hug. "Jane is hero for killing Ivan. Save all those women."

"Saved myself, as well. It *was* self-defense." She extricated herself from the Savchenkos' arms and brushed a lock of hair from Lana's face. "Take care of yourself and that baby."

When the brother and sister had left, Jane perched on the arm of Tim's chair. "Ivan's accomplice that night on the docks, the one you took down, turned out to be one of the bartenders at the restaurant. Ivan may have gotten him to do his dirty work with Natalya and Austin, too."

"Are you all right?" He ran his hand down her arm. "I know it's not easy killing someone, even someone like Ivan, especially the way you did it."

Sipping her coffee, she watched a hawk swoop through the air, maybe looking for prey. "I had to do it, Tim. He had a gun... Alexei was hurt. He would've killed all of us."

He pulled her into his lap, and she draped her long legs over the arm of his chair. "He made a big mistake punching you in the face."

"He did me a favor. That shocked me out of my stupor. If he hadn't hit me, maybe I would've remained frozen. Alexei would be dead, I'd be dead—" she cupped his square jaw and kissed him "—you'd be dead. I wasn't going to let that happen."

"Not to mention those poor women loaded into that container like cattle to the slaughter." He captured her hand and pressed a kiss against her palm. "Where did that screwdriver come from? I know we picked up some tools along with the safety gear, but I don't remember that you had it in your hand when Ivan had you at gunpoint. That part's a blur to me, as I was trying to figure out a way to take out his legs before he could shoot you."

"Irina gave it to me." Her lips twisted into a smile.

"Irina? The only one who wasn't completely out of it from the drugs? How'd that happen?"

"She didn't exactly give it to me. She just reminded me that I had it. I'd stuck it in one of the gaps of the container when I stooped down to look for the release for the door, sort of like a beacon to the captives to let them know there was someone on the outside working to free them. I forgot it was there. When Ivan had me up against the container, the gun to my head, Irina wiggled that screwdriver into my back. When I felt it, I realized it was the only way we were going to get out of there alive."

"Then we owe Irina, too." He curled an arm around her waist. "The Bureau is more than grateful for what you did, Jane. I think you're looking at a commendation."

"I'm glad someone likes me."

"The guys in the department can't actually be giving you grief over Damon, can they? That guy made a mistake and paid for it with his life. That's not on you."

"Just a few snide comments about who my next partner is going to be. Turns out Damon was providing tips to Ivan to protect Sissy—or at least he thought that's what he was doing. Ivan threatened to traffic Sissy if Damon didn't do what he said, but Sissy was never in any danger."

"I can't imagine that woman being anyone's victim. She's as tough as you." He squeezed her waist. "Are you going to be okay at the department?"

"I think the more my fellow detectives find out about what Damon was doing, the faster they'll come around." She flicked her fingers. "I don't care about their opinions, anymore. I don't have anything to prove to them."

"Anyone would be lucky to have you as a partner."

He rubbed her back. "I've never worked with anyone better."

"But now that work is over." She snuggled deeper into his arms. "Is our relationship destined to be tied to our work?"

"As fantastic a partner as you are, Jane, I never want to work with you again. This relationship is destined for greater things than that."

When his lips met hers and her heart soared, she knew exactly where this relationship was headed... and she was going along for the ride, full speed ahead.

* * * * *

Don't miss the final book in Carol Ericson's miniseries, The Lost Girls, when Malice at the Marina *goes on sale next month.*

And be sure to check out the previous books in the miniseries:

Canyon Crime Scene
Lakeside Mystery

Available now wherever Harlequin Intrigue books are sold!